FLIP-FLOP

A collection of short stories

Highly Commended Stories of the KepressNG Anthology Prize LILY 2022

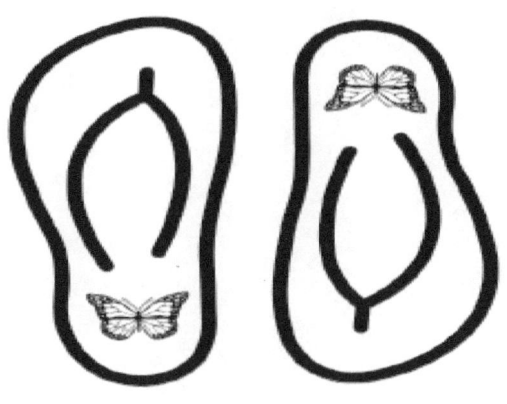

FLIP-FLOP

A collection of short stories

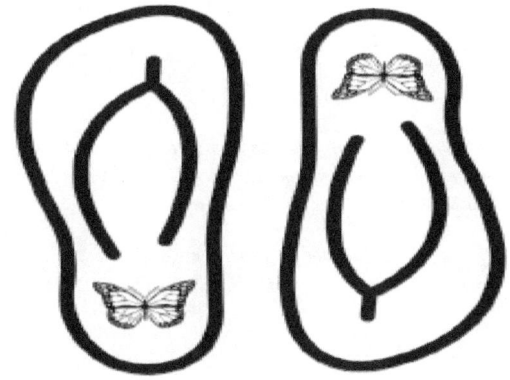

NIGERIA | UK

First Published in 2022

The moral rights of the authors has been asserted.
Individual contributions ©2022

This book is sold subject to the condition that it shall not, by way of trade or otherwise, be lent, re-sold, hired out, or otherwise circulated without the publisher's prior written consent in any form of binding or cover other than that it is published and without a similar condition including this condition being imposed on the subsequent purchaser.

Kemka Ezinwo Press Ltd (KEP) has no control over or responsibility for any author, third-party websites, or articles that may be referred to in or on this book.

A CIP catalogue record for this book is available from the Nigerian National Library & the British Library.

978 978 790 463 3(Paperback)
978 978 790 467 1(Ebook)

This novel is entirely a work of fiction. The names, characters, and incidents portrayed in it are the work of the author's imagination. Any resemblance to actual persons, living or dead, events or localities is entirely coincidental.

Typeset by Kepressng Ltd
Cover design by Chimele Ezinwo of Chigirl Arts

To

All who believe in change.

All who made this book possible.

Welcome!

This is the LILY version of the KepressNG Anthology Prize 2022.
The theme, REBIRTH, was to accentuate the need to survive. We're coming out of the COVID era, which has marred our adventures, livelihood, relationships, etc. for more than two years. We look forward to renewed friendships, hopes, and ideas.

We had ten (10) winners and more this time. These are the best ten after the winnings were collated. Interestingly, the stories were mostly about healing and in some sense coming of age.

Our judges were:

Efe Ogunnaiya is otherwise known as @bookreviewbymo on Instagram. She is a financial adviser who started her literary career reviewing e-books to feed her passion. So far, she has edited over ten books and two short stories which have become instant sensations.

Titi Oyemade enjoys reading and listening to music. She is currently a book reviewer for the Businessday Weekender newspaper, and her reviews have also appeared in The Newcastle Review website in the United Kingdom. While browsing the bookstore for books by Nigerian authors, a memoir, biography, or autobiography will almost certainly entice her into a reading binge. She owes her reading addiction to her book clubs, The Book Club Lagos and the Sunshine Book Club Lagos.

Agnes Kay-E is a Nigerian based in England and the author of eight books, including Blossom in Winter, a bestseller. She writes contemporary women fiction, fantasy, and new age fiction. Her latest is Anatomy of Harmony. She is presently working on another Contemporary Fiction. In her spare time, she sings and writes music.

Some stories in this collection have been previously published in various anthologies and literary journals. Their original appearances are as follows:
"The Fallout" in *The Aftermath* and in *Rebirth*

I am grateful for the opportunity to share this story with a new audience in this collection.

CONTENTS

Welcome! 1
REBIRTH 3
THE RAINBOW THAT GLOWED AT NIGHT 5
OUT OF THE PANG 9
RAISED BY MY THOUGHTS 19
MEL NEEDS A NEW NAME 27
NICODEMUS 45
EVERY STORM IS HOPE 60
THE GIFT OF THE RAIN 68
REBIRTH'ED 75
THE FACELESS KILLER 95
BONUS STORY 109
THE FALLOUT 111
OTHER KEP TITLES 134
CONTACTS 135
ABOUT US 137
2026 ANTHOLOGY 138

REBIRTH

Shalom Grace Omondi

I stand.

I stand on my roof. I stand on the edge. My hopes and dreams cry a song of agony. What could they possibly want? Are they not tired of my unfulfilled promises? I wrestle a mighty match with sanity. Why would I do this?

Perseverance is a great factor. A factor I do not have. I try not to overthink, but things may fall apart. Right now, they're falling. I will pick them up when I can (I want to). I could have been gone by now. Was this time wasted or a life recovered? I step down. I have not decided yet.

I will buy a notebook today and fix myself. This is a rebirth. As I walk, a car passes me, and I think again: I could have been gone by now.

Greatness takes time, and I hate that. I hate how I've not yet finished writing this, I hate how I might not finish it, and I hate how nothing is ever finished. Unless, of course, you finish it. I am so high up. I seem normal, but I am far, very far.

Would heaven take in a lost soul? I am not lost on earth, but I will inevitably be lost once I am not here. Yes, I will inevitably be lost. Would God want such hysteria in his kingdom? I want to go to heaven so that I may be born again and never have to repeat rebirth. I am an ethical woman. I will do it here on earth, considering I am not going to Heaven any time soon. It isn't impossible, at least, not for me.

I got my notebook, and I have been writing; I write for a few days and then stop. Then rebirth. It all feels like a loop. You fall, move, fall, and, of course, move. The fall is a great place to be when you have felt the ground before. It can be terrifying, but an overlooked part of rebirth is the "re-". There will always be a "re-", so you might as well get used to it.

I could have been gone by now, but I am not. A life recovered.

THE RAINBOW THAT GLOWED AT NIGHT

Rose Wangari

The sun sat hidden behind the clouds. She was not sure whether to completely peep out and shed her illuminating smile to the earth below.

There were no children playing outside. The bikes, skates, skateboards, rollerblades and hoverboards had been tucked away in the basements. There no longer were voices of children playing tag, hide and seek, hopscotch, skipping rope or hula hooping on the lawns or thoroughfare.

The mothers were no longer lingering on the drive to speak to their neighbours. Everyone seemed to love keeping in their houses.

The trees and the grass appeared to have stopped growing. There were neither squirrels nor chipmunks hunting for nuts. The trees had none to offer. The shrubs were not flowering. The buzzing bees and the butterflies had all disappeared.

The weaver birds were no longer having animated

conversations as they tried to outdo each other with their meticulous weaving. The rooster had altered his wake up *kokadodoo*. He was getting it out all too late.

The sun, moon, stars, clouds and the rainbow had a meeting one dull afternoon.

Do you see what I see?

What has happened to the world?

The children are not coming out to play. When they do, it's only for a few minutes, dashing back into the house without mingling with another. It seems they are trying to avoid each other.

They put on masks on their faces. They are not talking to each other. The best they do is a quick wave as they pass each other at a distance.

The sun spoke out, "I was made to give light during the day. I smile down to the earth, and everything gets warmed up."

The moon retorted, "I was made to light up the night. My gentle smile gives the people, plants, and animals a gentle and quiet night."

"I love it when you do not smile so hard at night. The boys and girls love looking up the sky for me, count my numbers before they fall asleep," the stars spoke shyly to the moon.

"I bring down the rain when I am too heavy. I make the plants grow for the people and animals to eat. I give them water to drink," the clouds added.

"Hmmmm! How about me? I bring a smile to the world when the sun and the rain are trying to outsmart each other. I am the peacemaker here," the rainbow giggled as he swept his hands across.

"I see you have been meeting without inviting me. You have forgotten that you need me? I better go my way," said the wind sadly.

"No! No! Don't go. We couldn't find you anywhere. You know you are all over the place. We are sorry. Please, stay and help us through," said the rainbow.

The sun, moon, stars, wind, clouds, and rainbow were all quiet for a while after explaining to the wind why they were having a meeting. Each looked lost in their thoughts.

Suddenly, the rainbow shouted. "I have an idea. Since we are all concerned about the human people, I will not only smile when the sun and the rain are fighting each other, but I also want to smile when the moon and the stars are sharing their space at night."

All the elements agreed.

That night, the rainbow smiled. It made the sky so beautiful.

The other elements hid behind the rainbow. They waited for a while, not even knowing what they were waiting for.

Soon people started streaming out of their houses to watch the spectacle in the sky. House after house, children, parents, and pets came out to look up at the sky.

The birds started singing; the scavenging little creepy-crawlies were out making their calypso song.

There were voices of children running around.

Finally! Everyone chatted, watching the sky.

The moon smiled all night and the nights that followed.

The sun smiled in the day.

How wonderful it felt to be of help. Thanks to the elements, the masks were taken off, and life returned to normal.

OUT OF THE PANG

Walusungu Nyachikanda

Three steps away from a shattered window stood Kayla Brown. She watched her close friend Hussein, drenched in human blood, call for help. The streets of Dehkanville were never the same.

One bright Sunday afternoon, Miss Brown made her way to her favourite coffee store, where she would wait for her close friend Hussein Mella. Hussein was a mischievous little boy with an IQ too high for his age. He loved exploring the world and getting into lots of trouble. Hussein was a few inches taller than Kayla and a year younger than her. Kayla considered Hussein to be her little brother and her best friend.

Hussein and Kayla went to the same elementary school in a small town called Dehkanville. Dehkanville was known for its amazing green parks, clean tarred streets, huge mansions, and friendly compatriots. Hussein believed that the best way to live life was by following your instincts and not following any rules or instructions. On the other hand, Kayla found it cool and did precisely what Hussein told her. Before she knew it, they had gotten into so much trouble by the time they had reached seventh grade.

Kayla came from a humble background, and her family condemned unruly behaviour, illegal practices, and dark humour. Before Kayla and her family moved to Dehkanville, they lived in a small cottage on the outskirts of Beldala on the east coast. She found it hard to make friends because all the children at her school looked different from her and came from high-class neighbourhoods. Moving to Dehkanville gave her a chance to start her life over.

"Ready for another day of horseplay?" asked Hussein as he got on the school bus and approached where Kayla sat. "I don't feel quite well. Today is my mum's birthday, and I promised her to…" Kayla said in a sad low toned voice facing the window.

"…so, does this mean our friendship means nothing to you? Huh?" Hussein interrupted Kayla in an aggressive tone.

Kayla stood up and made her way out of her seat. She quietly went and sat at the far back corner of the bus.

Hussein remained in his seat selfishly frowning and wrinkling his face. Little did he know that Kayla's mother was ill, and this made Kayla even more depressed.

Five minutes to the end of gym class, Hussein got into a fight with a little girl the size of an elf. He accused her of stealing his gummy bears from his backpack. Hussein expected Kayla to jump in and help him beat up the little girl, but Kayla just sat there in her tiny gym shorts and watched as Hussein punched the little girl in her face.

"Stop! Stop! I took your gummy bears. It was me!"

Everyone sighed as Hussein slowly took his hand off the little girl and stared at Kayla.

"I was hungry. My mother couldn't…" Kayla murmured as tears rolled down her face.

Hussein gave Kayla a stink eye and interrupted her, saying, "I hate you; I wish you would disappear." Hussein felt embarrassed for what he had done to the innocent little girl but still went ahead and yelled at her.

Kayla went home in tears, blaming herself for everything that had transpired at school. She ran upstairs to her mother's room and did not find her mother lying on her bed. She remained puzzled, wondering where she could have gone. Kayla took a shower and had her supper while waiting for her mother to walk through the front door. Kayla fell asleep on the living room sofa, and a few hours later, she heard the doorbell ring. Kayla quickly got up and ran to the door. She saw red and blue lights filling the empty house, and she could hear sirens coming from the outside.

Kayla's mother taught her to always ask who was at the door before she could open it to see who was there.

"Who is it?" Kayla asked loudly.

"Kayla? " You have to open the door, okay?" said a man dressed in orange overalls with reflective markings, holding a red helmet.

"I will, right after you tell me who you are!" Kayla yelled.

"Kayla, sweetie, mummy needs to see you. " Don't be afraid, okay?" the man said, leaning forward. "Get your coat and put on your boots. We will take you to mummy, okay?" the man went on as Kayla became quiet. "Kayla, honey? Are you there? Okay, so we are coming in to get you, okay?" the man shouted.

Kayla ran upstairs and did as she was told. The man rang the doorbell for the last time. Kayla opened the door slowly and told the man that she was ready to go.

It was too late; Kayla arrived at the hospital and saw her mother screaming in pain. Kayla screamed out, 'Mama,' more than once, but her mother could not hear her. Kayla, being only ten years old, did not know what to do. Silence reigned through the hospital hall as Kayla's mother stopped screaming and closed her eyes. Kayla ran into her mother's room, but a nurse stopped her. It was at that moment that Kayla knew that she was alone. She knelt and cried, "No! Mama, mama! Wait!" The nurse tried everything to resuscitate Kayla's mother but to no avail.

Six years passed, and Kayla had become much older and even more independent. Her close friend Hussein had become even more protective over Kayla and helped her overcome the trauma of losing her mother.

Unfortunately, Kayla started doing drugs, stealing, and even bullying innocent people. Hussein had been to jail more than twice, and not once did he ever feel the need to change his ways.

On the fifth of September, Tuesday morning, Kayla and Hussein went to the central park and were planning their summer vacation when two girls walked past them. The two girls talked about a famous actor who would be visiting their town in just a few days.

Hussein told Kayla that he had heard about the actor's whereabouts and that the actor was very wealthy. Kayla started to cook up ideas of how they would kidnap the actor, hold him hostage and demand a huge ransom money from his family. Hussein loved the idea but knew very well that it would be a scary and risky task. Despite that, Hussein and Kayla agreed to proceed with the plan.

Monday evening, Kayla and Hussein snuck into an old church building that Kayla had planned to vandalize. When Hussein walked in first, he saw a brownish wooden bookshelf at the entrance covered in dust and spider webs. He took a closer look at the bookshelf and discovered his father's name carved on the left side of the shelf. He wondered why his father's name was inscribed on that item. Hussein grew up without his father, and every time he wanted information about him, his mother and everybody else in his family said he did not exist.

Kayla smashed the shelf with a baseball bat and hit

it until scattered wood pieces remained. Hussein did not want to go ahead with their plan to vandalize the church but hesitated when he saw how much fun Kayla was having. He later joined and vandalized half the church when they heard coming sirens outside. Kayla quickly grabbed Hussein's hand and ran towards the back door. Hussein did not look all happy about what the two had done, but he overlooked the feeling and continued with his daily life of mischief.

The day came for Kayla and Hussein to execute their plan to kidnap the famous actor. The plan had backfired when Kayla told Hussein that she was not feeling too well. Hussein did not hesitate to cancel their plan because Kayla's statement had given him a flashback of what tragedy occurred in seventh grade. On the other hand, Kayla found her mother's old diary in the basement while cleaning the house. She began to read it, page by page, and to her surprise, her mother was not any different from how Kayla was as a child.

Kayla began to reflect on all the trouble she had caused and the pain she had put other innocent people through. She quickly grabbed her phone and dialled Hussein's number, but the phone rang and rang. She found that unusual and gave up on calling him but sensed that something was wrong. Five blocks away from her house, she heard people yelling and screaming in angry voices. She figured that it was just people protesting, but the voices did not seem to disappear. Kayla did not seem comfortable with the noise, so she decided to go and check on the commotion.

She got on her bicycle and rode towards the voices. When she arrived at the site, she saw a man standing on the front porch of his house, trying to calm the crowd down. The man resembled Hussein, but Kayla did not bother to approach him to ask further questions. The man was the one in charge of the old church that Kayla and Hussein vandalized a few days back. The town's folk wanted to know what happened to the building. Kayla stood in silence as she watched the people yelling and asking questions. She expected to see Hussein amongst the crowd, but there was no sign of him. She then moved away from the crowd in search of Hussein.

Hussein had gone to a neighbouring town to buy firearms that he intended to use in the kidnapping of the actor once Kayla felt better. Upon arriving at his apartment, Kayla had fallen asleep by his front door when Hussein woke her up and asked her to go home.

Kayla did not listen to him and decided to resist his grabbing. "I don't want to do drugs, steal or bully people anymore," Kayla said.

In confusion Hussein stared at her. "Did you drink anything today?" he asked with a giggle.

Kayla then sat down on the porch bench and told him to hear her out. Kayla began to explain to Hussein why she wanted to change and live a normal life.

Hussein disagreed with her and laughed at her theory. He later warned her to stay away from him and that she should never try to brainwash him ever again.

Kayla was disappointed at her lame attempts to help Hussein realize his wrong deeds.

Hussein told her that she would eventually go back to her old ways. "I'm going ahead with the plan. Meet me at 6 p.m. tomorrow if you are interested." Hussein said as he slammed the door in Kayla's face.

Kayla left his place, devising a plan to save Hussein.

The next day at 6 p.m., Kayla was nowhere to be seen. Hussein decided to execute the kidnap on his own. Meanwhile, Kayla went to visit the man who resembled Hussein, and when the man mentioned his name, Kayla figured out who the man was. She told the man everything that Kayla and Hussein had been doing and what Hussein was about to do.

The man was hurt and broke down. "Kayla, where is my son?" asked the man in tears.

Kayla decided to take the man to Hussein, but on their way to where Hussein said he would be after 6 p.m., they heard gunshots. The man quickly asked Kayla to hide behind a water barrel. He took out his emergency hand firearm in defence and protected Kayla, who was not armed. He stood firm and patiently waited to see who was exchanging gunshots. He was astounded to see Hussein and two other older men chasing after him.

The two men were the famous actor's bodyguards

and did not look like they would show Hussein any mercy.

Hussein's father tried to intervene, but Kayla jumped in front of him and asked him not to, then called out to Hussein, "I have found your father!"

Hussein shot one of the men, and just when Hussein tried to run, the other man pulled the trigger aiming in Hussein's direction.

Kayla ran inside a house that was damaged by the gunshots. Hussein's father jumped in front of Hussein and took the bullet instead.

The bodyguard got away while Hussein was left with his father's bleeding body in his arms. Hussein screamed and shouted out for help. Kayla stood by the shattered window, frozen in shock. The police, a fire truck, and an ambulance arrived at the scene in a trice. Hussein was arrested, and his father was rushed to the hospital. Kayla could not hold back her tears; she asked to go to the hospital with Hussein's father as she watched Hussein being put into the police vehicle.

Unfortunately, Hussein did not get a second chance to see his father. Immediately after his trial in court, he was sentenced to fifty years in prison with no possibility of parole. Hussein's father recovered but passed on three weeks later. Kayla was left all alone again. She vowed never to go astray or let anybody else close to her lose their way. She frequently visited Hussein in prison and took food, little notes, and school assignments.

Kayla became an advocate for all troubled children

and worked hand in hand with different psychologists, elementary and high schools, and juvenile prisons. She began sharing her story with the world on live television and radio to help change many hearts and help save lives. Kayla also shared Hussein's experience in prison to create awareness. Many children vowed to never become mischievous and that they would change for the better.

Years later, Kayla graduated from Rosewood University with a master's in psychosocial counselling and built her own therapy firm for troubled children in Dehkanville. By the time Kayla turned thirty, she had changed over three million children's lives and lived on to save the generations to come.

Walusungu Nyachikanda lives in Livingstone, Zambia. Her activities include Entrepreneurship, photography and Choreography. She enjoys writing stories that are fictitious which depict real urban life. She participates in classical music, Chess, badminton and basketball and adventure trips. I also enjoy reading and writing poems, books and short stories. I started writing stories when I was in primary school.

RAISED BY MY THOUGHTS

Maryam Dalhatu

She'd cracked a few bones. The baby was halfway there, but the guilt came first. First, it was her mother's voice, then the loud voices of the honking cars nearby. Now it's her head pounding, her breath seizing. You dare not call heartbreak a pain if you've never witnessed real turmoil.

The nurses were yelling now. "You will die if you don't push."

Amina had heard how women die during childbirth, and this passed some shiver down her spine. Now she's yelling, giving her all into this one tiny life that is worth fighting for.

"I am tired," she cried.

"The head is already out. Let go one more try, pusssssh," the doctor's voice finally came.

Amina knew that having a baby wasn't a piece of cake, but having one with a broken wrist was just a harder task. Funny enough, the pain in her hand didn't bother her one bit. It was invisible. After about an hour of intense battle, with tears as her companion and a sharp pain in her head, a faint cry came.

"It's a boy. A champion," the doctor said.

"Alhamdulillah," Amina managed to whisper, but that wasn't all. The cry started to fade out. She could see the doctor's face between her thighs; she was shocked.

"What's happening? What is wrong with my baby?" she panicked.

"Don't worry. I will handle this," she heard the doctor say before a loud pain knocked her unconscious.

"Madam. Madam..." the nurses rushed to her, and within seconds, she passed out.

Amina was a feminist to begin with, and coming from her religious perspective, it was scarce. She lost about four proposals because of her nonchalant attitude and lectures about how women should be independently happy.

Her first love, Sadiq, left her after his mother asked her about her view on being a housewife. As expected, she gave her a candid view regarded as 'disrespectful'.

Her second was more of a believer and too religious for her liking. He laid more emphasis on heaven than on earth.

Her third, a prince named Abdul, was so hot-tempered he slapped her once for talking to a guy in his presence.

The fourth Zakari was more of the opinion that women are meant to be in the kitchen. So archaic.

Then came her prince charming, Isa. They've been married for a year now, and things went smoothly until recently, when he asked her to quit her job to take care of their new baby when it arrived, and since that day, hell went loose.

She woke up still with the pain in her head, ears, and wrist. 'Awwwwwww' words finally freed her mouth. Her eyes caught Isa, and he smiled sharply.

"Where is my baby?" She tried jumping out of bed, but pain and her husband's fast fingers drew her back.

"Relax, he's fine."

"I need to see him," she pushed up again.

"Amina, I said he's fine," Isa yelled back.

Her eyes met his, and she felt a little bit of relief.

"Mrs Ibrahim, how are you doing?" the doctor asked, walking in.

"I'm fine. My body feels like hell."

"I know. Having you in for delivery after an accident was..." She looked at her and her husband and nodded with a smile.

"But you'll be fine. Luckily, we saved both of you. Since you're conscious now, I'll have the nurse bring in your baby," she added.

"Thank you, doctor."

"Now, can I check your pulse?"

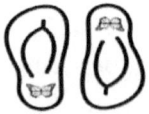

Isa grew up in a more busy area, or rather the 'ghetto', though he wasn't one of the street kids because his father was a retired police officer with a duplex. He got everything he wanted. Not necessarily everything, but he was comfortable. Happily comfortable. His mother was the problem. She always wanted him to get richer, marry into a rich family, or do something to make him famous. On his hand, simplicity was the key and then came Amina, who recently got a job in his office as the Secretary. She looked materialistic at first because she had this funny way of talking with jokes and intriguing stories. He was on level 9, and she was on 7. They met at the office canteen during lunch hour. She left her purse somewhere and couldn't find it.

"Can I pay tomorrow? I can't find my wallet."

"I'm sorry, ma, my madam will not allow it," the lady's voice came.

"But you know me, I buy food here, every day. I can drop my desk address. Find me there if you think I will run, or I will drop my I.D. card or something, please."

"No need for that," a male voice interrupted.

"How much is the meal?"

"It's two thousand naira only, sir."

"Here, take."

Amina smiled, embarrassed.

"Thank you for..."

"Don't thank me," he interrupted with a quick smile and made for the door.

True love does happen, and love at first sight exists too, you know. We live in a world where trauma and scary beliefs keep us tied down to our mistakes. We do not want to break through and prosper.

The nurse walked back in, holding the baby in a light blue towel, or what do parents call that thing again? Amina smiled, and she gave a big sigh of relief.

"Alhamdulillah."

"I told you he was fine," her husband said, collecting the tiny human.

"If you need anything, ma, let me know," the nurse smiled and went for the door.

"People sure do smile a lot around here."

"Oh, Amina. Stop being sarcastic," Isa mumbled. He sat gently on the edge of the bed where she was and showed her the face.

"He's so handsome. Look at the tiny nose. For a moment, I thought I was going to die in there."

"Can you be positive, please?"

"I've always been. This isn't one of those discussions where we end it in a quarrel haba."

"Calm down, please. The baby is here now, isn't it? Relax and enjoy the company, please."

"I'm always the negative one," she murmured.

Amina became fond of him after that incident. Though he was really quiet and reserved, not as loudmouthed as she was, their time together was rather smooth than hazy.

She looked into her baby's eyes. He was smiling.

"Toothless," she giggled.

Life is a journey of truth and daring, and finding someone worth risking all for is the main deal.

"Abba," she called.

"Yes, dear."

"You know what just ran through my mind?"

"This baby here, this moment, this is more magical," she said, looking at him.

"What's wrong, dear?"

"Nothing. I was just thinking about how we will do this parenting thing. I never thought of it this way, you know. It was more than just being pregnant for nine months and having a fractured wrist at the end. It's sacred."

"Babe..."

"Let me finish, please," she interrupted.

"I am better than this. We all are. I know we've had countless arguments on this, but right now, right here, this baby just gave me a second thought. I think… I know I'll be a great mother and a greater woman if I accept my mistakes and take corrections. I said I wouldn't quit my job for no reason, but this child here is not just an opinion to gamble on. This is a rebirth of destiny, our rebirth. I love and cherish you for giving me time to be me," she finished with tears in her eyes.

He held her hands tightly.

"Thank you for giving me something worth fighting for."

MEL NEEDS A NEW NAME

Favour Martins

Dear Mr Davies,

I am writing this long letter to you because I am certain about a few things. You see, I have had doubts about a lot of things. I have stood on the thin line between atheism and Sunday school. I have written a thesis I wasn't sure of and have swallowed the pill of uncertainty life gives to all of us. So, when I tell you I am sure about this, you should pull your socks up, roll up your sleeves, put on those reading glasses you use only at the office and read this.

I am writing this because Mel needs a new name. I am sitting at my dining table, the one with nothing that relates to food but everything that screams books. Books on psychology, the human mind and therapy. This paper is balanced on the scaffold of my copy of Dorian's book on psychology. I have just eaten a bowl of cold spaghetti; I had to eat it cold because I know that if I had warmed it, the intensity with which I write this letter would be reduced, pulverized even.

Today was the fifth therapy session with your daughter Mel. The fifth time, I sat across your daughter, trying to reach into her soul.

All the things I have come to know about Mel are stored in an amber coloured jar in the recesses of my mind because I want to prevent any kind of effervescence.

Can I tell you something?

I used to love writing when I was younger. It started with a longing to talk to someone, anyone, about the insecurities I faced. There was no one, and so I began to keep a diary. That diary was the closest thing to a video of my entire life while I was a teenager. I wrote about the days when my Mum left me for Kano to run her many businesses; I wrote about the uncertainties of not having a father, the struggles, and the many questions that ravaged my mind. I wrote poems, too - poems of longing and sunset. Mel reminds me of the poems I used to write. Disjointed, strewn about like the body parts of my mum as she lay dead in Kano. An arm here, a femur there, a rib forcefully jettisoned from its initial position, grotesque. Those were the saddest days of my life, you know; I was burning hot with revenge for the people who had killed my mum. Those were the days I stopped writing, too – life, so fickle, was not worth writing about.

I remember the first time Mel walked into my office. I knew that instant that she was distinct. First, I did not have my ten minutes of clearing-my-head time; she came at exactly 3 p.m. I must tell you why that stood out to me. Since I came back to Nigeria to practice after college, I have worked with a rigid routine. I get to the office by 9 a.m. I have my first session by 10 a.m.- after an hour of yoga and mind prepping- till 12 p.m., after which I have a lunch break. The second patient comes in by 1 a.m. and leaves by 3 p.m.. The third person comes then till six pm. All the patients scheduled for the sessions do not come at the exact time, so I have time to clear my head after a frustrating session of probing and thinking and getting ignored. There's always a ten-minute break cut out by the universe for me. Mel came at exactly 3 p.m. It was the second reason I doubted she was Nigerian or even African.

Our first session was different from the usual cold, deathly stares I get from patients. I didn't expect a patient to be so chatty. Her calmness was ostensible. She wore tight denim and a big T-shirt. Her flat black shoes walked around my office, observing, looking at pictures and the artwork in the left corner of my office room. She read the 'Say no to depression' tag off the flier pasted behind the door. She touched my flower vase and commented about the lavender's almost wilting state. She was like a house owner who was observing her new house, savouring every moment, anticipating the memories she would make there. I watched her breathe in the air in my office and then signalled for her to sit.

"I hate sitting," she said almost immediately. It

came as a shock. My mind was already beginning to search for a diagnosis, physical appearance, gait, and gestures.

Maybe she needs sedatives, or she's mentally deranged or schizophrenia... no, I think it's bipolar disorder; I mean, she's starting to get aggressive, I thought.

"What's your name?" I asked as soon as she leaned forward on the chair in front of her.

She didn't reply; her eyes were on a picture above the mini shelf on the right. I followed her eyes; she was looking at my framed certificate.

"Where are your parents?" I finally asked.

"Parent," she cut in. "He's not here."

"Okay."

"What is your name?"

I had decided to give the usual advice: eat well, exercise, sleep well and take your pills. (I would prescribe depression pills; the commonest mental illness young people suffer.)

"Mel Davies."

I looked up. She was definitely Nigerian; the tan skin, kinky hair and plump body couldn't have said otherwise.

I had already started writing to Melissa before I asked what Mel meant.

"Melancholy," she said almost immediately.

I was stunned. I know Nigerians give their children very strange names; I have heard about a couple who named their twins Trust and Obey and another couple who called their triplets Miracles, Signs and Wonders because they were given birth to during a church programme which had the theme; Miracles, signs, and wonders. But Melancholy, I have never heard that.

She saw my expression even without looking at me

"I get that all the time. My name has a story."

I was dying to hear that story, but I didn't want to pry

"You schooled at Pennsylvania? How impressive!" She said, with her eyes still on the framed certificate.

"Why did you choose to be a therapist?"

I looked from the paper where I was scribbling my inferences.

"I did not exactly choose it. I just needed to do something with my degree in psychology here in Nigeria, and since I didn't want to teach, I decided to be a therapist."

"How old are you?" she asked again.

I paused for a bit; nobody asked their therapist this kind of question.

"Thirty-five," I said, cringing for the question that always followed how old I was, the question about my husband.

"You're a miss," she said and then smiled.

"I am twenty-two," she said and then looked at me.

"Why do you think you need therapy?" I asked.

"There's is something growing in my chest."

I stared at her with furrowed brows. I scribbled 'confused state' on the sheet.

"How do you know something is growing in your chest? Should that even be true, you do not need therapy then; you need a surgeon."

"It's like a tumour; it was this size before." She raises a fist to me and continues, "Now, I feel like it's going to explode any moment from now, like a tsunami."

"That still does not explain why you need therapy."

"It metastasizes, but this time, not to distant organs but to people."

The first thing you learn about therapy is the act of being calm. I tried hard to keep it all in, to understand this girl that knew everything about tumours and how it relates to therapy.

She smiled then, like this was a sport she liked, reciting gibberish to therapists and watching them cringe and think and watching the hollow spaces in their mind expand and expand, and then she spoke;

"In plain words, I bring bad luck."

I looked at her intensely, trying to pick out something, a peripheral inkling, something that pointed to the fact that she was out of her mind.

She was calm, her eyes fixed on mine, like they had told her that there was something in the eyes of a therapist that took away your fears and problems.

"What is my diagnosis and treatment?" she asked after a few minutes of my staring at her in absolute confusion.

I thought about what to say. There is no medical

definition for bringing bad luck to people.

"I am not sure," I said honestly. "I think we need to reschedule while I do a little research on all you have told me."

She turned to leave.

"Mel? Can you call me later today?"

She turned back and looked at me with that peculiar, unreadable expression. She took my card and then opened the door to leave.

Mel did not call me.

Mister Davies, I must say, your daughter's eccentricity tugs at a person's mind. It folds itself into a slight weight that sits in your heart, runs around your floors, and stains your walls like a two-year-old. I thought about her while I cooked my meal that night, in my car, as I waited for the Apapa Expressway traffic to dissipate.

One morning, a bird perched on the rail in my corridor. It was yellow. So Beautiful. It stared right in the eye and surveyed my corridor. It saw the loneliness that plagued me, the pin drop silence that engulfed my apartment. It flew away with all it had garnered from me, from my flat. It would take it to its flock, chirp about a lonely sick woman it had met; they would laugh, scorn, and maybe cry for me. I wish I had someone to talk to about Mel that way, except for my stucco walls and large television.

Our second session was hasty. I was pissed with how cheery she seemed. She asked endless questions like I was a transparent wall, and she could see the loneliness that had eaten deep into me. I wanted to ask about her friends, whether they gossiped about therapists with their noses stuck up in the air, feeling like they had the answers to their problems.

She came again, by 3 p.m..

I had just finished a session with a boy who had obsessive-compulsive disorder. He had started by picking up my pens on the floor and shifting my books, like something in his mind screamed 'clean, clean, clean!' I had allowed him to do his bits and then prescribed the same pills. It was obvious he had been skipping his pills.

Again, I didn't have an answer to Mel's problem. Her session was last, so I carried her with me as I walked the lone street to my apartment; I thought about how not-in-need-of-therapy she seemed.

I had gone home that night to stalk her on social media. Her Instagram account was private, and I couldn't risk giving her the impression that I was stalking her. The headlines would read 'Therapist is a serial stalker', and a lot of people would even read 'serial killer'. I had put off my phone in frustration.

Our third session was the beginning of an unplanned friendship. The details of that day are imprinted in my mind like the creases on my Palm.

"Why do you think people come late for events and hide their lack of punctuality under the shadows of 'African time'?" she asked.

Sorry to digress, Mr Davies, do you know your daughter is really smart? Sometimes, I want to ask her the questions for IQ assessment, but I fear she would figure out somehow that those questions are not related to her condition.

"I think it's because they know that those events do not start at the time they say they would." That was the only logical answer I could give.

"So, what happened to waiting till the event starts? What happened to putting your thoughts together, surveying the environment, and taking deep breaths?"

I stared at her, at a loss for what to say.

She brought out her big pink journal, the one she scribbled things on as we talked, the one I yearned to read.

"I have a theory about African time," she said and chuckled.

"People love African time because they are afraid."

My confusion was visible.

"They are afraid of being alone," she continued. "The event organizers are afraid of conducting an event for only themselves, and the guests are afraid of staying alone. It's a kind of phobia. I would look it up and tell you during our next session."

Mel's mind is a mine, one that is unreachable and untameable.

"What phobias do you have?"

"I fear water."

"Why?"

"Something so free has got some nerve. It reminds me of something I can never be."

I stared at her in utter disbelief.

On the days before our sessions, I walk around with my mind in my hands; I flip and flip through memories of past therapies and classes I had taken while in college. I was looking for something that could click, anything that could lead me to the solution to Mel's problems. Anything that could maybe sate her for a while before I had time to refer her to somebody else. Nothing made sense; depression didn't cut it, nor did bipolar disorder.

I must confess, she made me read a lot. She made me search for answers to mundane things, everyday events, and people's eyes.

I guess that's what happens when a person gives themself over to you. You are engulfed by their identity, so much so that it is intertwined with your own. Therapy is the result of empathy, after all. But this - this is not empathy at all. It is a kind of intersection I cannot quite explain.

It was during our third session that she told me about you. It was a fluid conversation that somehow had you as the epicentre.

"Are you happy?" I had asked her.

"What does that mean?"

"You don't understand the word?" I had asked, clearly confused.

"Abstract nouns are variable, I don't know how you define happiness."

Resigned, I mumbled, "Okay, are you sad?"

"I don't know either."

"How do you feel then?"

"I feel like my life is moving slower than I am."

"How?"

"It feels like I'm putting on a magnifying lens. Every detail is intensified, every experience is imprinted in my mind like an office stamp."

"So, you remember all experiences clearly?"

This was my chance! I would pry now.

"Do you mind talking about some of them?"

"I miss my dad," she said after a pause that seemed like forever.

"Where's he?"

"I don't know. He's like water."

"You don't live with him?"

"I live alone. He lives with his new wife."

"What about your mum?"

"She's gone. She died as soon as I was born."

"Oh my, I'm sorry."

"My name is Melancholy because that's how my dad felt after I was born."

I could not believe that at all.

She talked about you. You used to love her in bits. In small portions. A love that was short-changed by grief and anger. Sometimes, when you were on a high, you showered on her all the leftover love from your dead wife. When you were pissed, she was a distraction. You would stare at her as she tried hard to get your attention after you came back from a long day at work. In your relationship with her, she was a shadow, a docile receptor of whatever you gave to her.

Her days at Federal Government College Ojota were a phase that led her to the realization of this deadly thing she spreads to people. The days when she sought love in the arms of naive JSS3 classmates that hedged her in gave her a place to be. The day when they had read Tim LaHaye's why you act the way you do. That day, everyone screamed that Melancholy was sanguine and laughed. She had retreated into her shell. A carved out safe space in her mind. There, she was not Mel the San. She was a seven-year-old princess, laughing through the darkness of the world, playing with sand houses, and building blocks.

She had walked around in that shell from then, and that was when the tumour started to grow.

Ekanem, Mel's best friend, committed suicide. It was during one of the school's inter-house sports competitions. All students were to go to the sports field. But there was no Ekanem with her long strides. Ekanem ran a hundred metres in one breath like she was rushing through life, like a clock in her head ticked faster than life itself.

They got to her room on time, and the sight sent screams ringing through the entire school. Ekanem was lying down on the floor, with a bottle of cyanide pills emptied by her side. Ekanem of gummy smiles and math wit.

Mel would see her shadows on the walls of her heart. Mel would weep and think and then hold the pain in her hands like hot coals. Too afraid to hold too tight, too cautious to let it go.

How could a person be best friends with someone else and not know when they were on the brink of slipping into darkness? Weren't friends supposed to share burdens, encourage each other, and dispel every sadness? She had cried herself to sleep every night. If only the tears would wash away the images in Ekanem's eyes that had shone like stars in a dark sky.

When Mel told this story, we were sitting on the reclining chair on the balcony of my apartment. The sky was a bright blue, and the world was quiet except for crickets and owls. She had come to visit me for the first time ever, and we had started talking about a lot of things. I had told her about my mother and her horrific death, and she had listened intently. Her eyes shone with tears; the wind carried my voice high and low. First, a crescendo and then a diminuendo, like the high-pitched soprano voices that sang in the choir in the Anglican church I attended as a child.

When she finished her story, it was dark. The blue clouds had gone to sleep and, in their place, a grey blanket littered with a gazillion tiny stars and the half-moon casting a shadow of two women sitting side by side, crying.

We stayed that way for almost an hour before I took her into the sitting room. We slept on the couch; each person rocked to sleep by her own demons, by all the memories we tried to forget.

On our fourth session, she told me why she had gone to a lot of therapists since she was nineteen. It was after her breakup with Dare, her first boyfriend.

They had dated for one year. It all ended with Dare's mother coming to her hostel in her second year at the University of Lagos. Dare's mother was sophisticated, but the fetters of stereotype and religious superstitions still held her bound. She had come to warn Mel to stay away from her son. "A child who kills her mother and friends should not be married." She had said.

Dare came later as if cast under his mother's spell. He told her he'd been hearing a lot of rumours about her – that she killed Ekanem. Mr Pelumi, the corper who was close to her, was accused of raping students and sacked; she had destroyed her roommate's relationship with her boyfriend with her evil charm. She. Was. Evil. Dare was hurt that he was hearing all of this from outsiders and not from her. He was sorry, but he could not continue the relationship if she would not be honest with him. She had gone home that night to an empty house. You had either gone to the houses of one of your female acquaintances or slept in your office. She had stayed outside the house and shed silent tears.

After Dare's breakup, she started giving all of it a lot of thought. She started with Google. What she discovered was that Google had no answers for a person in need of redemption. After a long search, she came across tumours in a medical journal she picked up while waiting to see a therapist, the third she had consulted. It said tumours were neoplastic cells which had lost their apoptotic abilities and now multiplied unregulated. She had gotten interested almost immediately. They talked about benign and malignant tumours. Malignant tumours were the ones that metastasised to distant organs and caused death faster. She read about women with breast cancer and mastectomy.

That night, when she went back home, she examined her firm breasts in quadrants, as the journal had said. She checked for any lump, anything that proved she had a tumour. She stopped when there was nothing. She had then googled tumours and read up on them. This was the only explanation for the symptoms she had. The fact that she felt anyone that much as stared at her twice was going to be knocked down by the drunk driver of a trunk the next second. She repelled people; she was tired of running from all the things that haunted her. It was easier to stay alone. She was not afraid to be alone anymore. That way, she was safe.

The therapist's obsession had begun as a need. A need to talk, to be friends with someone that was not exactly a friend. She had read that tumours only spread to organs that were in a person's body, that is, her friends, people she had given her tumour-ridden heart to. Seeing therapists was a way to outsmart the tumour; she could talk, visit, and spend time with people who were not her friends. The tumour would not spread to them. It would lie in wait for its prey, the people she called friends.

Mister Davies, I know you dream of a day when your little princess will be swept off her feet by her

Prince Charming. I know you are enamoured with the aroma of party jollof rice filling up the hollow spaces in your house, sticking to your mind and slowly evolving into sweet ecstasy. She would either marry a therapist or ride through her life with the recklessness of a vehicle with a faulty brake.

Today, during our fifth session, I called her Melancholy instead of Mel. I saw that cursory cringe, the sadness that engulfed her as soon as I said the name. It was like a being that had exacted its presence in our midst. It came with a silence. I stared at her, how different she looked from the girl that walked into my office at exactly 3 p.m., the girl that was not afraid of being alone.

She looked small, defeated, docile. And that was when I found it. What I had been looking for all along. Since our first session, I had not prescribed any pills for Mel or written down a diagnosis. But then I saw it, through those eyes that have lived through the pains of twenty-two years in a world that was too fragile to have her.

Diagnosis after five sessions: Mel needs a new name.

Let me tell you what a name does to a person. It is inhaled like the hot balm my mum used to massage when I had dislocated a joint as a child. It is then carried into the sinuses and hair tips of the nostrils. It goes to the lungs later and then is transported like oxygen from the high-pressure alveolar blood to the less-concentrated tissues. It invades the tissues fast! It feeds off blood, water, and serum, all the fluid the body produces and is then excreted. The process happens again when the name is called, and the neurons fire instantly to make the bearer of the name answer and inhale again.

I know this is complex. Well, that's what you get from medical school, plus studying the human mind.

A name tethers a person to the place where it was first uttered. It invokes a presence just like the one at the office today. It takes a person and makes that person something big, bigger than the person's will, a child of the universe succumbing to the will of the name. It has a mind of its own and breathes on its own. It is a bespoke identity that a person does not have the right to change.

Have you read Mariama Ba's 'So Long a Letter'? I read it as a fourteen-year-old in secondary school, and all the while, I wondered why a person could write a letter so long it would fill a book. I know why now, looking at this letter that holds the sacred parts of your daughter, the tiniest details of her life. It's fascinating how you can become so deeply involved in a person's life, live it through yourself, walk through their memories, and see their fears firsthand, only to start matching their life with your own.

I write this letter because sometimes, I am Mel, bound by the demons of my past and choked by the fierce arms of loneliness. I write because if a person comes to you seeking redemption, you have to save yourself first and then bring them to a place where what they seek is a river. They can drink to their fill and even have their bath and create a home with the foundations reaching into the depths of the river. I'm writing because the path to Mel's rebirth can only be lit up by you.

The world needs a new Mel, one that is afraid to be alone, that comes late for events and makes friends and satisfies the sanguine fire that burns inside of her. Mel needs a new name.

I hope this letter meets you well. I hope you shed small tears for your little girl. She's so pretty and so small. I hope you carry her on your shoulders until she learns that her life is hers to have and own and live.

Love,
Miss Okorie
Mel's Therapist

NICODEMUS
Rigwell Addison Asiedu

You stabbed your best friend three times in his abdomen, and afterwards, you ate pizza with your bloody hands. The cheese and sausages were warm in your mouth, and you relished the smell of the hard bread base. You licked your fingers and the tomatoes on them mixed with the blood. You sat on your chair long after you were done eating. You watched the blood ooze out of Moses as he lay on the ground, with his face turned sideways in an awkward manner.

His mouth was still open, the way it had been when you first stabbed him, and shock shook him. He looked funny with his crooked teeth exposed for the world to see. You had always teased him about his teeth. Now he was dead, murdered. You were the murderer. You loved how the light left his eyes, like a lantern dimming into darkness. It was so glorious watching him die.

You had to get rid of the body. You were not bothered about getting caught. It wasn't the first time you murdered someone. It wasn't even the tenth time. You had lost count. You killed for fun. But killing Moses was not the usual pattern. He deserved to die for what he did. It was unforgivable. He was crying when he came to you this evening. He said he was so sorry. You took him to the kitchen and wiped his tears with a tissue. Then you said you were too tired to cook and ordered pizza. The pizza delivery man arrived, and you even smiled as you brought it inside to be devoured. But you saw Moses sitting at the table, not crying anymore, and rage made your lips quiver.

"You should still be crying, Moses," you had said.

"Nicholas, I am sorry. I know I have hurt you in an unimaginable way and -"

"You should still be crying," you said slowly and dropped the pizza on the dining table. The table shone with a polished brownness.

"I have changed, Nicholas. I have given my life to Christ. I have been reborn. I'm a changed man. That's why I'm telling you this. I couldn't lie to you anymore."

"You. Should. Still. Be. Crying." Your voice was hard as steel now. You were thinking of the shiny steel of your favourite knife. Knives had always been your favourite toy, even as a child. Your parents had thought you were demon-possessed, so they took you to prayer camps to pray for deliverance. The pastors and prophets declared that an evil spirit was eating your soul and making you heartless. That was why you enjoyed hurting other kids in your class. That was why you killed animals for fun and dug out the entrails with your hands. That was why at age thirteen, you tied your younger brother's legs and hands with ropes and pushed him into a swimming pool. You did that because he ate your fried rice and chicken without your permission. That was your favourite. You still wished your mother had not found him before he drowned. You wanted to enjoy the spectacle of him dying. Too bad Kwaku was still alive twenty years after. Well, you could still kill him. You hadn't forgiven him for eating your food. That was yours, not his. It was unfair that he wasn't punished. You loved punishments. You enjoyed being the punisher. The power of punishing was exhilarating.

Anyway, your stupid friend, Moses, had been punished, and you needed a way to get rid of his body. You took his phone. You needed to unlock it. You raised his lifeless finger and used it to activate his fingerprint and unlock his phone. Well, that was easy. You scrolled through his chats on WhatsApp. You tapped on the chat of the lady he had been trying to woo. He had told you about her. He told you about how he was crazy about Efia. He met her at a wedding reception in East Legon, and he quickly went closer to her to "shoot his shot". He got her number, but she had been playing the hard girl card, and it was proving rather difficult to convince her to go out with him.

You tapped on Efia's chat and quickly typed.

I don't think I can do this anymore. I'm tired of life, of chasing things I can never have. Nobody ever wants me. Even my parents abandoned me as a child.

I'm cursed. I'm tired of living. I'm ending it. That's the best thing to do.

You copied the message and posted it on his WhatsApp status. Moses' phone began to blare with calls and messages. You smiled and wrapped the body in a body bag and dumped it in the boot of your car. You drove to his house and took the body to the kitchen. You stabbed his chest with his own kitchen knife, and his fingers wrapped around it. Then you staged the kitchen to look like he died there. You rushed outside the house and sat in your car, preparing your body for what came next. Your body began to shake with sobs – they were rehearsed tears.

Your mind was formulating a story. You knew what to tell the world. Moses had been depressed. You tried to convince him to seek professional help. You saw his WhatsApp status this evening, and you kept calling him to talk him out of committing suicide. You rushed to his place, but when you got there. *Oh God!* When you got here, he was – oh God! Why did he do this to himself? You tried to help him. You did. And he pushed you away. You tried to help him. But now he is – *Oh, Lord of mercy!* Now he is gone!

You deserved to win an Oscar for your performance. Of course, Moses' loved ones believed you. Of course, the police believed you and your fabricated grief. You refused to eat for days, crying in your room. Your voice was hoarse from the howls, and your stomach growled with hunger. But you had to stick to the script.

"Nicholas, you have to eat," your parents told you when they brought you different meals.

"Mummy, he has been my friend ever since we were kids. We grew up together -"

"I know."

"Why—Why would he do this to himself? To me? I loved him as a brother."

"Take heart, Nicholas," Daddy said. "God knows the best."

Your brother, Kwaku, avoided you during the days of your mourning. He was still afraid of you, of what you could do. When he recovered from his close brush with drowning, he had begged your parents to send him to a boarding school.

"He is going to kill me. I can see it in his eyes, the way he looks at me. He is going to kill me."

The day Moses was buried, you finally bumped into Kwaku. He was talking to Efia. Your belly burned with rage as you watched him talk to Moses' crush. Late Moses. Duh. Moses had always been an early bird. Now he was late. Efia was laughing and leaning towards your brother. You wanted to bash his head against a wall. You walked up to them and smiled thinly.

"Hello, Nicholas. Kwaku here was trying to cheer me up with the story of how he tried to swim as a young child and almost drowned in the swimming pool," Efia said and gave a weak smile. Mourning looked good on her. Her dimples were conspicuous, and you wanted to stick your fingers in there. You wanted to use your fingers on different parts of her body.

You laughed and threw your head backwards.

"Yeah, I remember that day. He kept screaming, and I came around. I was so scared that I jumped into the water to try and save him. But I couldn't swim well, too, and we almost drowned together. Our Dad had to save us. Efia, Kwaku was vomiting fried rice in the pool. It's so funny, now that I think of it," you said and adjusted the edge of your black turtleneck.

"Of course, it was funny." Kwaku was looking at you directly, and you could see the cold animosity in his eyes. The story that both of you were telling was what your parents had crafted for the both of you to share with the world. They didn't want the whole world to know that they had a little devil who tried to kill his younger brother.

"I'm so sorry that happened to the both of you," Efia said and touched Kwaku's chest. You pressed your lips together, and your fingers stiffened with taut anger. Now that Moses is gone, Efia should be yours.

"I'm going to greet Moses's parents," Efia said, looking at the both of you. "I will be back."

You watched the roll of her buttocks as she sauntered away. You imagined tying her to a bed and whipping her naked butt with a belt until they were red. Then you imagined taking her from behind. Efia was yours to take.

"Stay away from Efia," you said as you stood

beside Kwaku.

"I should be telling you that, Nicholas. Stay away from Efia. You are just going to kill her the way you killed your last girlfriend."

"Cynthia was stupid. She slipped on the wet tiles of her room, and she hit the back of her head on the ground," you said and heaved. You wished you missed Cynthia. There was nothing to miss.

"That is what you made it look like. Too bad Moses had to go through suicide."

You smiled at distant relatives as they walked by. Kwaku waved. To the outside world, you were two nice brothers comforting each other on a dark day.

"I didn't have anything to do with this, Kwaku," you said.

"You think I'm going to believe you? C'mon, I know who you are. You are a psychopath."

"You shouldn't tell a psychopath they are a psychopath. You could be the next victim."

"I'm not afraid of you."

You smiled and moved closer to Kwaku so that your shoulders touched. He shuddered and moved away from you.

"I'm not afraid of you," you mimicked him mockingly.

"Please stay away from Efia," he pleaded.

"She is mine."

"She is a Christian. She goes to church. She led Moses to Christ. You can't do this to her. You don't even go to church. You don't even believe in God.

She doesn't yoke with unbelievers."

"Then I guess I would have to do some rebranding."

"What do you mean?"

You shrugged and watched Efia from a distance. She was hugging Moses' mother. The mother looked like a flower wilting in harsh sunlight.

"I will become born again, too. She will lead me to Christ."

"You can't be saved." Kwaku's voice was low. He kicked a stone. Dust floated above his feet, and the motes coloured his black shoes brown.

"C'mon," you said and nudged him with your hips. His body shivered at your touch. "God is ready to welcome all those who believe. I am a sinner, and I want Jesus Christ in my life. And Efia is going to lead me to him."

"I will report you to the police if you do this."

You turned and faced him sharply. Kwaku almost fell, but you held his hand and squeezed his fingers. You enjoyed watching him wince. He tried to withdraw his hand, but your grip was strong.

"I will kill Mummy and Daddy before the police get to me. I will chop off Daddy's toes and shove them into his anus. I will cut off his penis and shove it into Mummy's vagina before cutting them open very slowly. It's been my biggest fantasy. Don't make me do it. I know how much you love them. Don't do this to them."

Kwaku's eyes filled with tears.

"You can't be saved, Nicholas."

You sucked through your teeth and smiled like a child who had been offered ice cream. Efia's backside was quite impressive. It deserved to be whipped like a bad child.

"I'm Nicodemus seeking redemption." Your stare was blank and devoid of expression. You looked like glass. Sharp glass.

You visited Efia the next day at Tabora. Her house was just beside the Salvation Army school. Your shoulders drooped, and your face was plastered with snot and tears. When she opened the door, the worry on her face satisfied you.

"What's wrong, Nicholas?"

"I just can't stop thinking of how he died, how I saw him. I can't sleep at night. It haunts me. I should have done something, Efia. It feels like I killed him."

"You didn't do that. He did that to himself. You are not a murderer," she said and hugged you. You smiled over her shoulder. Of course, you were not a murderer.

She led you inside, and you talked about how you felt so empty inside.

"I keep thinking of where I would go when I die. I think of death, and I'm so scared. I deserve to burn in hell."

"God is ready to save you from the bondage of the devil. You won't burn in hell when you are saved." She began a sermon that made you yawn internally.

"You don't know the things I have done."

"We have all done bad things. But Christ came to die for our sins, to redeem us. No matter how bad your sins are, His blood can wash them away."

You held Efia's hands and cried.

"Efia, I want to be saved. I want Jesus Christ in my life."

"Thank you, Jesus." She pressed your fingers, and you felt electricity zap through your veins. Your manhood stiffened as she made you repeat the Sinner's Prayer, and she led you to Christ.

"Dear Lord Jesus, I know that I am a sinner, and I ask for Your forgiveness. I believe You died for my sins and rose from the dead. I turn from my sins and invite You to come into my heart and life. I want to trust and follow You as my Lord and Saviour."

"Come with me to church this evening," she said when you were done crying. You said yes as you wiped the tears from your face.

That evening was the first time you had been in church after so many years. You stopped going to church when you got to the university. You had always found it theatrical and unnecessary. Christians were fools beneath you. They didn't know what it felt like to live freely, act out your impulses, kill at will, eat at will, and have sex at will. They were people who had to submit to a fictional God's will. You almost yawned as you listened to the pastor preach about God's love and redemption.

"When you come to Christ, you are born anew. Old things have passed away, and you are a new creation."

"Preach on, pastor!" Efia hailed and clapped. You clapped and nodded with enthusiasm. You had to blend in, pass the test and win the girl. Boy gets girl. Men did all sorts of things to win the hearts of their desired ones. Ladies were cows to be wooed, instruments of pleasure to be used. That was what you believed. You knew Efia was a feminist; you had gone through her socials. She hated misogynists. Well, you would just blend in and be whatever she wanted you to be, so long as she also bent to whatever you wanted her to be. You would cook, do the laundry, take care of the kids, treat her like a queen and make her think she had a say in making decisions in the house. It was easy. She just had to be good. It would be a shame if it got to a point where you had to kill her.

The pastor called first-timers to come out and be welcomed. You told the congregation you were there to stay, and they clapped for you, welcoming you. You smiled shyly and rubbed your hands on your trousers.

"God, he is so handsome and shy," you heard the young ladies whispering. "I like him."

Fools, you thought. They were fools.

The pastor called you to his office after the service. The room was spacious, and the white walls irritated you. You hated anything white, that whole charade of purity.

"My name is Pastor Dennis Afoakwa," he said. "You are welcome to our church, Nicholas."

"Thank you, Pastor. And that was a great sermon. It was so powerful. I could feel the spirit of God speaking directly to my soul. I feel so different now that I have given my life to Christ."

"Do not be deceived. God cannot be mocked." The pastor's voice was low, and his stare was piercing.

You were taken aback.

"What?"

"You are not deceiving anyone but yourself. I know why you are here. I know who you are, what you are."

You laughed loudly and leaned back on the chair. You raised your legs and crossed them on the table.

"And what am I?"

"You know that yourself."

"C'mon, I came to church. I am saved. I want to be saved. God can save me, right? No one is beyond redemption. With God, all things are possible."

"Do you want to be saved?"

You looked at Pastor Dennis and whistled notes of Pharrell Williams' Happy.

"You said you know why I am here, so you should know the answer."

"Why did you kill Moses?"

You laughed and snapped your fingers to the music in your head.

"He was a member here, so you should know the answer."

"He came to you to beg."

"Wait, were you the one who sent him? Oh, you

did send him. Oh, that's sad. So, so sad. So you killed him."

"*You* killed him."

You snorted.

"He committed suicide."

"Why? Why did you kill him after he begged?"

"I told him to continue crying, and he ignored me. I hate it when people don't listen to me. Nobody ever listens to me. Everybody already thinks that I'm this evil, twisted monster, and I'm not worth listening to because everything that comes out of my mouth is a lie. Nobody ever listens."

"He was sorry for what he did."

"He raped my ex-girlfriend, Cynthia. He raped her, and I thought she was cheating on me all the time that she withdrew from me. He raped her and made her a shadow of herself. And I had to kill her because she was trying to cut me off. I didn't know she was traumatised. I thought she had seen that I was a soulless monster and was trying to cut me off. She wasn't listening to me. I begged her to stay. I... I... I begged her, but she didn't listen, and I had to kill her. I had to kill her because nobody ever dumps me. Nobody ever leaves me until I say so. Moses made me kill Cynthia. He made me kill the love of my life. He stabbed me in the back. So I stabbed him three times, and oh God, it was so glorious watching the shock register on his face, watching the light leave his eyes. He deserved to die."

"So, how do you feel now?"

You shrugged.

"The same way I felt before ordering the pizza that evening."

"How?"

"I felt nothing. I felt nothing at all. It was just silent inside me and hollow, like an empty drum. I don't feel things that people feel. I don't feel things that people feel I should feel. I feel like ordering pizza now."

"You want to kill me." Pastor Dennis's voice was low, and his sustained eye contact was unnerving.

You shrugged and leaned towards him. You winked at him.

"I *have* to. But I don't know how I would get away with it this time."

"Because you won't, Nicholas. Efia knows why you followed her to church. Your brother told her, and your parents know what you did to Moses and what you've threatened to do. We know everything."

"I could still kill you and kill myself afterwards."

"You are not going to do that."

"You talk like you know me."

Pastor Dennis leaned forward and supported his chin with his hands.

"I want to know you. I want to listen to you."

You leaned back and looked at the ceiling. You felt trapped. You thought of ways to get out of the situation, but your mind was blank. You were genuinely hollow inside. You could feel the vibrations of a higher power in this room. It made goosebumps rise on your skin. When you looked at Pastor Dennis, his lips moved in silent prayer. You could tell that he was speaking in tongues. Your stomach growled.

"I am hungry, pastor. I am ravenous, and I don't want the bread of life. I want pizza."

"Great, Nicholas. Let's order pizza," he said and picked up his phone, unlocking it with his finger. You tapped your feet three times on the floor and leaned back in the chair, closing your eyes. You thought of eating pizza with bloody hands.

Rigwell Addison Asiedu was born in Ghana in 2001. He was raised in Nigeria before moving to Ghana for his tertiary education. In 2019, he won the Dei Awuku Writer's Contest. In August 2020, he completed a scriptwriting course at Lagos Film School and now writes scripts for production houses across West Africa. His poems and short stories were published in the international anthology Musings in 2020. In October 2020, Rigwell published his debut novel, In Times Like These. In January 2021, he took a copywriting course at the Academy of Copywriting. Rigwell is a freelance writer, blogger, novelist, poet and copywriter. He is currently studying Communication Studies at Pentecost University, Accra. He published his second novel, Jollof Rice, along with a collection of poems, Vessels of Verses, in 2021. In 2022, he won the "Student Author of the Year" at the Pentecost University's SRC Excellence Awards.

EVERY STORM IS HOPE

Lynn Felicia Mbeiza

"Sometimes words are hard to find. Other times, they flow like the Nile pouring into the Mediterranean. How far I have come is just hard to fathom…"

I, Mukisa, was raped at the age of three. Or should I start more conventionally? Mukisa, which basically means' blessing,' and I guess I am one - we will get to that. I was born many years ago and bred in Katwe, a ghetto suburb in the heart of Kampala, Uganda. I am a lone child to my mother but the fifth and only girl of the known ten children of my father. Most people are not surprised by the brokenness and poverty of families in the ghetto, and my case is no different.

To be honest, I do not remember exactly when my mother left home. My memory only recollects the times I wondered. "Why on earth was I left here with a drunkard father and never-present brothers?" Why was I even named Mukisa if my mother could not see me that way? I was about to find out why she left, a reason I so remember very clearly- the rape.

I am now 20, pursuing industrial art and textiles in my first year of university. At 18, I sought to find my mother. My father had no clue whatsoever where she went. All he had left was a picture of her donning the beautiful *gomesi* with her hair well done, held in a ponytail. "We had an introduction ceremony that day," my father said. "My brother's."

My father went on to describe in great detail the picture. My mother's beautiful eyes, the beautiful *gomesi* that my father kept to this day, her benevolent smile that runs through his mind to this day. He also mentioned that I looked so much like her, something I did not see- at least from the picture.

With all my emotions high and my anxiety rising beyond control, I could no longer hold it in.

"Dad?"

"Yes, my daughter."

His calmness shocked me.

Prior to this event, my father, being a drunkard, was the tough kind. Not that he was violent- I surely cannot say that about him- but the tone in his voice always made us scatter. One day, after one of his drinking sprees, our youngest made sure not to return home for about two days. Reason? My father shouted at him for no reason. Oh, how that boy trembled!

"I want to know why she left."

"My mother," I added, just to make sure we were

on the same page.

"Are you sure you want to know?"

I have never seen my father cry. Not this hard.

"Go to hell! You need to be punished for your deeds."

My mother could not believe her eyes when she entered what she called her bedroom. We lived in a one-roomed house; at that time, a family of five and curtains held up using sisal-made ropes separated the sitting room from the bedroom. Without enough space, all the children, the boys and myself, slept in the makeshift sitting room while mummy and daddy slept in the bedroom.

That fateful day, however, my father invited me into their bedroom at about midday. I remember being so happy because no child had crossed the curtain to the bedroom side. He drew the curtain, looking around for anyone who might be watching.

"Your mother was at the market." His shirt was soaked in tears by now.

"And my brothers?" I asked, still choosing to be oblivious to where this conversation was going.

"I sent them out to play."

Bits and pieces of that day came back to my memory. My father had told me to take off my clothes and never to tell anyone. What happened next, I cannot bring myself to describe, but I needed to understand why a man I called my father had put me to shame.

Life was never a smooth ride for him. Like us, my father grew up in a one-room house with all five children and their parents. They did not have curtains to separate rooms. The poverty in their home caused both parents to work long hours, leaving the children mostly alone.

"All five of us started doing drugs, alcohol and copying…"

"Copying what?" I interrupted.

"The things we saw at night."

So, I was not the only victim! This hit me like a landmine. In fact, my aunt, their last born, was at a very young age introduced to sex by her elder brothers. I could not help but sob at the mere thought of the horror. My mind raced to imagine my uncles and father taking turns with this innocent girl. Oh, how she must have screamed for her dear life! But they could not stop.

My father and his brothers could not go a day, and when I was three, with my mother in the market and my brothers sent away to play, it was my turn.

"I'm sorry, my daughter."

But I still could not understand why. Why did he choose his only daughter? Why that particular day? He was normally away.

"I...I could not help it that day, I do not know what happened."

I stood up.

"We both know I was raped." My anger was at boiling point. "By you, my father, or are you even my father, huh?"

I did not let him speak. "So anha, what happened when my mother found you?"

"She left." That's all he could say before I stormed out of his house. Forever, or so I thought.

My mother had moved over 70km from Kampala. She now lived in the Masese landing site on the outskirts of Jinja city. Word had it that she had gotten married twice after leaving my father. She was unmarried now

After I left my father's house, my aunt, with whom we suffered the same ordeal, was gracious enough to take me in. The trauma that the various rapes, by her brothers, caused her to remain unmarried.

"Let me tell you, Mukisa, I can't trust a man."

I could tell. The woman was trembling. Goosebumps filled her arms, and she held herself together like a fetus in its mother's womb. She went on and on to recount her story and then.

"Every night...can we change the topic?" she asked. "I don't want to hate my brothers the more."

"Okay. Do you by any chance know where my mother is?"

My mother ran to her and stayed for a month after she left my father.

"I don't know, but she told me she had found a job."

"What kind of job?" I asked.

"Fishmonger. In Masese."

That was odd. From what I gathered, my mother did not know anything about fish. How did she even get a job that far at such short notice? I would later find out that she found solace in the wrong place - her brother-in-law.

I know this is a very long story, but I've also had a hard time telling it. You're curious, I know, but be slow; I'll tell you what happened next. Knowing that my mother had left my father, one of her brothers-in-law told her about starting a new life in Masese. It was all a hoax. He had taken her to Masese to marry her because he had always admired her.

I understood why my mother never looked back and never came back for her only child. Her husband, my uncle, threatened to kill her if she ever did. But why did she leave me behind in the first place? She also doesn't understand, she says. I don't hold her to that, either. My uncle later died, and my mother moved on to another husband who left her.

My mother will never return to my father as she chose to stay in Masese. My father still lives in Katwe with some of my younger siblings. My siblings, my elders, live the ghetto life; I'm the first to get to university. I happened to get help from different people along the way for my education. I hope to help my younger ones too.

My life after finding out about the rape was affected at first. I grew cold towards my parents - my father for lack of self-control and my mother for never turning back. But haven't I sinned myself? Wasn't I a wretch like them? I'm not as innocent myself! I needed money one time, and I turned to prostitution at 17 without the knowledge of my father! Does he know that now? Most likely not. Does God know? He does but, in his mercy, chose to change my life at eighteen just before finding out about my rape. I'm now a changed, regenerated person, and I pray that God will soften and change my parents' hearts one day.

I don't necessarily want to tell this story. On the contrary, I could be silent, but that doesn't help. I need people to understand that certain circumstances are not the end of the world. Yes, not all is well because my mom has not forgiven my father yet, but I have found peace in forgiving my parents. My dad for the rape and my mom for never looking back. I recently started a nonprofit based in Katwe to help people battling rape, drugs, and alcohol.

Now. If this is not rebirth enough, I don't know what is.

Lynn Felicia Mbeiza is a twenty-four-year-old with an overpowering interest in writing. Besides writing, She's a nurse and a Christian.

THE GIFT OF THE RAIN

Eyinlojuolodumare Ajayi

The wind blew as she made her way to the never sleeping city of Amity, carrying the distant barks of dogs, the screeching of cats, gunshots, distant screams, and other questionable sounds. She tugged lightly at the dress of the lone figure who made her path far from home.

Her name was Stephanie Samuel, and she was tired of life. She was a fifteen-year-old and a broken girl despite what people thought. She usually smiled even in pain, but now she was done pretending she was ok. She thought of her troubled childhood as she wallowed in self-pity. She was never a Samuel from birth. She was adopted after her own parents abandoned her, and it was all because of that stupid and degrading incident.

At the tender age of six, she was raped by her seemingly favourite uncle. Despite his numerous threats, she reported him to her parents, but alas, they blamed her for what happened and deemed her promiscuous. They decided they didn't want a defiled daughter, so they dropped her at an orphanage and ran away. After all, they can still make more children. If only they knew. They even forgave her mother's brother for defiling but detested the defiled.

Stephanie felt her whole existence was a lie. She became numb and almost emotionless. If her parents could give her up like that, then she must be a terrible daughter though she still didn't see what she did wrong. She was quite surprised when she was adopted barely six months after being left there. It was while growing up that she began to realise how wicked her biological parents were.

Living with the Samuels was a whole different thing. They couldn't have a child, so they decided to adopt. They saw her broken soul through her eyes and decided that they were going to shower her with all their love. She didn't understand this. She thought that they were playing with her emotions. She thought they were pretending to love her, so when she opened up, they'll break her as her parents did and toss her away. After all, they weren't her birth parents and are bound to do worse. She didn't know she hurt them by calling them Mr and Mrs Samuel instead of Mom and Dad because she was too busy waiting for the day, they'll throw her out, but of course, that day never came.

She couldn't stand the fact that they still loved her, so she did the next unreasonable thing she could think of. She ran away. This explains the reason why she was on the streets. She had planned it for days, but it was pretty evident that she didn't plan it well as she didn't have any destination in mind as her cold attitude earned her no friends, and she couldn't go to a family friend's house as they will contact her adoptive parents. She didn't have any cash in hand or food or water or clothes. She only left with the dress she was wearing.

The wind picked up as it became colder. Stephanie could smell the rain in the wind. She shivered and looked around for shelter. She didn't have an umbrella or a blanket to keep her warm. Thunder struck immediately; it began to rain, forcing the girl to the nearest shelter, which happened to be a church holding a vigil.

To anyone observing, she was a latecomer who barely escaped the rain. She sat on a pew in the back row in order to avoid attention to continue wallowing in her whirlpool of pity and didn't expect the next thing she heard.

"There is someone here in this service who has been hurt by the ones they love."

She looked up to see the preacher giving his ministration.

"That person no longer feels alive and now that person is running away. But running can never solve your problems. It will only compound it until it becomes too much to bear. Running away means that you have accepted defeat without even trying. It means you have given up hope. But I want to say to you this night that there's still hope for you because there is someone who will do anything for you."

There is? Who? She anticipated what he was going to say next.

"His name is Jesus. Everyone say, 'Jesus'!"

She hissed in disappointment as people chorused 'Jesus'. Saying she has not heard of him is a lie. She never went to church as Mr and Mrs Samuel were never religious, but she had heard about him from school and roadside evangelists who shared tracts that she ends up throwing away the minute she got the chance to. They all talked about Jesus like he was some kind of superhero. She couldn't wait to get out of the church.

"Well, I know that you are in doubt, but Jesus knows and loves you very much."

She was stunned. How can someone I don't know, know me, and still love me and why does it seem like he is talking to me.

"The Bible says in Psalms 27:10 'When my father and my mother forsake me, then the LORD will take me up.' Do you know what this means? It means that God will always be with you.

Jesus is the Son of God who came to the earth to die for all our sins because he loves us all. John 3:16, 'For God so loved the world, that he gave his only begotten Son, that whosoever believeth in him should not perish, but have everlasting life.'

So till today, we exult God the Father, God the

Son and God the Holy Spirit. The Holy Spirit is the comforter whom Jesus said he was going to send to us as he went to heaven."

So he left us? But why? she thought.

"He has gone to prepare a place for you and me in heaven."

Really? But I am a sinner, she thought sadly.

"We may think that we don't have a chance but Romans 5:8 says that 'But God commanded his love toward us, in that, while we were yet sinners, Christ died for us.' If you allow Jesus in your life, all your sins will be forgiven and forgotten because our God is a forgiving God. All you need to do is let go of your past and your pain.

Leave your sorrow and shame and let God grant you eternal peace. Jesus will make you happy and give you a new life so it's up to you to accept Jesus as your Lord and personal Saviour.

He was bruised, beaten, and pierced for our sake. So, give your life completely to God and allow Him to revive you. If you are yet to be born again, come closer and allow Jesus to direct your everything.

2 Corinthians 5:17 says 'Therefore if any man be in Christ, he is a new creature: old things are passed away; behold, all things are become new.'"

Stephanie believed all that was said. There was a supernatural being who loved her more than her parents to even die for her. She didn't know when she stood up and walked toward the preacher until she was close to the altar.

He looked at her and smiled knowingly. "Repeat after me," he said.

She repeated the words, "Dear Lord Jesus, I know I am a sinner. I believe You died for my sins. Right now, I turn from my sins and open the door of my heart and life. I confess You as my personal Lord and Saviour and I ask you to be my guide for the rest of my life. Amen".

Immediately, she felt calm within her. She realised that she had been crying but they were tears of joy. She was given a new start. A new slate. A rebirth. The entire church prayed for her.

The Preacher whispered to her; "They are waiting for you."

Immediately she ran out of the church. She got to her destination and realised that the rain had stopped like it was never pouring. She hesitated before knocking on the door.

A very worried Mr Samuel opened the door. "Stephanie, where have you been? Your mother and I have been worried sick. We were about to get the police involved. We thought we lost you..."

Stephanie cut him off with a hug.

Mr Samuel was shocked as she had never initiated any form of physical contact with him or his wife, but he embraced her and brought her into the house.

"Stephanie, where have you been?" her mother said upon sighting her. "Are you ok? Are you hurt? Did something happen? Talk to me, dear," she probed.

Stephanie smiled, "Mummy, I'm sorry for worrying you and Daddy. I promise I'll never do it again."

Mr and Mrs Samuel were shocked but elated. She finally accepted them as her parents. They hugged her as they let their tears flow.

"I love you."

Eyinlojuolodumare Ajayi sings, dances, write poetry and stories, draw, codes and makes crazy but useful accessories for myself when I need of an item. She is a Jill-of-all-trade-Mistress-of-all with a spontaneous creative streak.

REBIRTH'ED

Esther Alex

"Argghhhhh!" Her loud, ear-piercing scream woke up Nina, who was sleeping soundly beside her.

Nina sighed in understanding as she turned to stare at the distraught and scared-looking Dami as she tossed all around the bed, sweating profusely.

There's no doubt that she just had another episode of a nightmare from her painful past.

"Dami! Dami!!" She tapped her lightly, her mind overwhelmed with pain and pity for the twenty-year-old beauty beside her.

"No! No, please don't do that. Let me go, okay? Mum! Mum!" she screamed, as she suddenly sat up on the bed, her eyes wide open in horror.

The inexplicable nightmares due to a terrible experience she encountered as a young child of seven were set to torment her forever.

Every other night as she grew up, she suffered the same fate. The monster that did that to her was still living fine and well, even married with kids.

She was diagnosed with PTSD - post-traumatic

stress disorder – when her parents took her to a psychotherapist.

Dami slowly looked at her elder sister, who was sitting up and watching her with worry and anxiety clearly written on her face, and a pool of tears immediately clouded her eyes.

"Nina, I... I..." She broke down in tears.

Nina reached out to her and pulled her into her embrace, tapping her back gently as she whispered into her hair.

"I know. It's okay."

She could only burst into another fit of tears as she cried more, her tears pouring down in torrents on Nina's shoulder.

"Dami, it's good to see you all grown up. Wow, Mommy Dami, your daughter is getting prettier and prettier daily. Are you sure she's only seven?" Uncle Madi, as he was popularly called by the kids, said playfully to Dami's mom, hiding his evil intentions beneath the facade of a gentleman smile as he stared at the young and innocent Dami.

He wasn't just an ordinary visitor. He was someone familiar to the family and also lived in the same neighbourhood as they did.

Mrs Tina laughed at Uncle Madi's remarks casually and excused herself to get him something from the kitchen.

"Dami, stay right here and play with Uncle Madi, okay? Let me get him something to drink," She

instructed.

Dami nodded obediently, even though she stared sceptically at this visitor. She thought he was rather strange and didn't feel comfortable with him.

Watching her retreating into the kitchen and out of the backyard, Madi couldn't conceal his urge again. He drew closer to the edge of his chair and leaned closer at the prey he was set to devour, his eyes brimming with a devilish lust.

He's a paedophile, but of course, no one in the neighbourhood knew.

Seeing his reaction, Dami, although really young, knew she wasn't comfortable with this uncle. She looked away from him in the direction her mom went.

She and her mom were the only ones in the house as her dad was yet to return from a trip, and her elder sister had travelled a few hours ago.

"Dami, come here," Madi said as he reached out to touch her.

The little girl stared reluctantly at him before slowly climbing down from the three-seater couch she was on.

His eyes glowed widely with unspeakable intentions and expectations as he watched her every move keenly.

Dami stared once more at him and decided she wouldn't go to him.

Instead, she turned in the direction her mom went to and walked two steps that way when a pair of strong hands suddenly grabbed her.

Next, she was on the lap of this strange uncle. Naturally, she tried to climb down from his body, but his firm hands kept her in place.

"Uncle Madi, I want to go meet my mummy," she said as audibly as she could.

But the ferocious beast ignored her, smirking maliciously as his right hand made its way into her flared skirt from underneath her legs.

Startled by his sudden action, Dami struggled hard once more to climb down, but she wasn't successful. She could only resort to one thing.

"Uncle Dami, what are you doing? Let me go quickly. I want to meet my Mommy."

"Shush! Your Mommy is coming soon. Be quiet."

He hurriedly shushed her as his fingers soon located her pants.

He slowly parted it aside and just as he was about to insert a finger into the vagina of the young child, she bit on his shoulder.

He was startled by the sudden sharp pain he felt so naturally; his grip on her loosened a bit.

Dami took her chance and quickly slipped away from him.

On seeing her about to escape in the direction her mom went, he was scared out of his wits, and he hurriedly grabbed her again, clasping her mouth tightly in case she tried to scream. His determination and devilish intent are stronger than before.

In her dilemma, she couldn't understand what he

wanted or what he was doing, but she knew his intentions were bad.

"Mmmm...ommm! Mommmy!"

She tried to scream, but her screams came out as inaudible moans because of how tightly he was closing her mouth.

Soon, a low, painful, restrained sound emitted from the mouth of the bewildered little girl. Her eyes bulged, and her body stiffened as she was overcome with terror and shock at the pain in her private area. Madi was successful in his purpose, adding a low, satisfied, animalistic sound, ignoring the horrified look on her face and the tears pouring down in torrents.

It wasn't the first time he was indulging in such acts. He would be fine as long as no one ever finds out. He thought he heard her mom's approaching footsteps. Suddenly, he tried to coax her into keeping quiet. With a threatening look, he promised to beat her up if she told her Mommy.

"You mustn't say a thing to anyone, or I'll flog you and do this to you again, understood?" he warned, putting on a terrifying expression to deter her from disobeying in case she thought of it.

Terrified beyond measure, Dami hurriedly nodded her head obediently, not daring to entertain thoughts of telling her mom again.

Nina cried silently as she watched her only sister weep convulsively in her arms. She regretted the reality that she wasn't around when Dami got sexually abused. If she could go back in time, she definitely wouldn't dare to travel to her aunt's place that day and would stick to her sister all day and chase the bastard out of their home immediately after he had stepped in.

When Mrs Helen returned to the living room, she found her little daughter sitting far away from her initial position, looking extremely grieved with a tear-stained face and a little fluffy toy in her hand. As a mother, she instantly felt something was amiss.

She looked over at Uncle Madi; he was sitting and operating his phone casually. He looked up immediately after noticing her presence.

"Ah, Mommy Dami, good thing you're back. Dami started crying after waiting for you for a short while and not seeing you. She refused to play with me, so I gave her a toy to play with," he lied with a sweet smile.

On hearing this, Mrs Helen felt relieved and smiled at her daughter.

"Dami, come over here. I'm back now." Mrs Helen walked to her daughter, effortlessly picked her up, and then placed her small body on her lap.

Dami looked away from him immediately after catching his threatening and terrifying glare, remembering his promise to do that painful thing to her again if she should dare tell her mom.

She hurriedly wrapped her tiny arms around her

mom's waist as though she was afraid she'd leave again and buried her terrified face in her chest, wanting to cry but not daring to.

This Uncle had even just lied easily to her mom without any fear; how much more terrifying could he be?! She wondered.

"Uncle Madi, thanks for looking after her for me. I had to go out and send someone to help me get the drink; we ran out of soft drinks yesterday. Sorry for the delay," Mrs Helen said with a casual smile.

"Ah, hahaha," Madi laughed pretentiously. "You shouldn't bother, Ma. Thanks, but I have to hurry home now. I was just informed about an emergency meeting at the office," he lied effortlessly, standing up hurriedly, not wanting to spend another minute there as his purpose was already accomplished.

"Oh! In that case, it can't be helped then."

Dami watched her mom exchange pleasantries with the wicked uncle but couldn't say a thing. She was glad he was leaving, and she knew within her that he was someone she'll forever detest.

After that incident, she became withdrawn from everyone and was scared of every little thing. She became extremely timid and would cower or burst into tears at the slightest rebuke.

Her nightmares began from that day and every

other night, her terrifying screams would wake everyone up. When asked what the problem was, she would only shake her head and cry, not admitting anything was wrong with her.

After many attempts to coax her into talking failed as time went by, her parents could only resort to prayers and even took her to a child psychologist.

For over six years, the trauma of that very day tormented her in the form of nightmares to a point she was losing her sanity and soon got diagnosed with PTSD.

Another painful year went by, making it seven years before she finally began to react to treatments and was gradually getting better. The nightmares had significantly subsided; only then was she able to tell her family what had happened to her as a child.

Mrs Helen was so aggrieved, bitter, and vengeful that she couldn't forgive herself.

Her family wanted to take revenge, but the evil man was now married and had long relocated from the area.

Mrs Helen couldn't forgive herself more because she had been relating well with the enemy who caused excess misery to her family and had even attended his wedding.

She wanted to avenge her daughter and deal with that ferocious monster in human skin, but there wasn't anything she could do. There wasn't any evidence to their claims, and this happened a long time ago.

Her family could only trust God to reward him

accordingly. They were grateful Dami was becoming better again.

All was fine until when Dami got into a higher institution, already nineteen and was returning from a late evening tutorial session alone one day, she suddenly got apprehended by several guys and was almost raped. If not for the timely intervention of a stranger, she wouldn't have bothered to see and would have only run for her dear life.

Since then, her nightmares have returned. She became depressed, extremely timid, and easily scared again. Her trauma returned, and her hate for the opposite gender increased greatly to an unspeakable extent.

Being a beautiful girl, naturally, many guys couldn't keep their eyes off her, and this fueled and increased her hatred for them. She wasn't psychologically sane anymore.

Sleeping at night was an immense war. Sleeping during the day became regular. Night, in itself, became a horrifying existence to her.

She kept to herself and refused friendship with others; tears were her daily companion. A few times, her elder sister, Nina, would come to stay with her in school.

The few times she went out, to avoid the attention of the opposite gender, she'd either dress in big outfits, wear face caps and nerd glasses, or wear a scarf or a hoodie.

When we walked, her eyes were always on the

floor; she was famously known in her environment and school as the weird girl.

Dami ran away from people who tried to befriend her and would rather stay alone all the time. She was in her final year now and would be sitting for her final exams soon, but much to her despair, her condition was still the same, and she wasn't improving; rather, she was getting worse.

She was tired of life and extremely sick of her existence. Her life was now hanging on a thin thread; at any moment, she might just give up.

Dami was tired of being a burden to her sister, she was tired of making her parents worry.

On many occasions, she had contemplated suicide, but she had also given up on the idea because she knew deep down that it wasn't the best option. Doing that will only make her family feel terrible and guilty, and that's something she wouldn't want.

She'd only promise herself to continue to push through even though she didn't see any meaning to life again. She knew she just had to survive, no matter what.

Nina knew just how her sister felt; she just prayed her desires were granted soon, and her parents' constant prayers would yield results. Her beautiful younger sister was in a mess because of that one evil man. How badly she wants to end his miserable life, but that wouldn't benefit her in any way; it would only make it easy for him to leave earth without being punished.

She desperately wanted to see her sister living. The quenched fire that once lit up her pretty dove eyes many years ago wasn't there anymore, and she wanted it to return.

They've tried all they could do for Dami to be healed, but their efforts won't pay off if she wasn't willing.

Dami was far from being psychologically sane now. It'll take only the divine intervention of God to heal her perfectly and bring her back.

Nina sighed again as a tear slid down her chin.

Weeks went by quickly, nothing changed for Dami except that Nina had already returned home, and she was alone again.

On a weekend of one eventful morning, she set out gloomily as usual for a nearby supermarket. She was out on most of her provisions and foodstuffs.

Dressed in her usual weird outfit, an oversized white hoodie over a long flared floral gown, her fluffy flip-flops, a small backpack, and her black headset, she walked down the street while listening to the loud but soothing music from her headset. The volume was extremely high as she didn't want to be concerned about any sound coming from her surroundings.

Soon, she took a turn down a quiet street, but at that very moment, something extraordinary struck her, causing her to stop suddenly in her tracks, leaving her stunned for a while.

That sound...

How am I hearing it? Where is it coming from? she mused.

Taking a sharp, deep breath, she inhaled and closed her eyes; then, she listened again to ascertain the source of such a mysterious sound. Definitely, it wasn't coming from her playlist. She'd never heard anything so soothing, assuring, and melodious as this mysterious humming sound.

She raised her hands to her head and removed her headset, letting it fall to her neck. She listened again, turning swiftly in the direction she felt it was coming from.

This mysterious sound felt like a companion to her; it felt as though it was communicating with her and understood all she'd been through. Tears flooded her eyes instantly, and she felt a sudden urge to cry just as her legs moved, and she began running in the direction of the voice eastward.

This humming sound was more mellifluous, captivating, and harmonious than the sympathetic vibrations of a local flute.

As Dami ran, the sound became louder and louder. Thoughts on how she's hearing this sound from a long distance away, even when her headset was playing loudly in her ears and shutting her from every other sound, didn't matter to her as she was only concerned about getting to the source of such outstanding and soul-soothing music.

Something exploded within her again, and she felt a sudden chill around her; she knew then that she'd found the source.

The air around her felt extremely different but strangely comforting.

Sitting under a tree in a quiet garden with his back to her was a young man, playing softly yet intentionally on a keyboard in front of him while humming mysteriously, an extremely soothing but unexplainable tune with such confidence and a deep concentration. His composure made him emit an aura so powerful and not relatable to this world but of another realm, which Dami felt was heavenly.

Overwhelmed with a powerful feeling of submission to this mysterious force, Dami felt an indescribable sense of relief and euphoria wash through her. Her heart felt like it would burst anytime soon as she watched him play, while the tears clouding her eyes gave way and ran down her cheeks in torrents.

Sensing her presence, the young man turned and flashed a breathtaking smile at her and said in one sentence.

"Welcome. I've been expecting you."

Dami couldn't hold back herself again as her knees grew weak, and she gave in totally, falling on her knees and bursting into tears.

Her tears held unspeakable words she couldn't say, the pain she'd endured, the feelings of depression, all her pent-up emotions of fear, anger and despair, the feelings of being abandoned, the shocking, mysterious relief she was feeling now, and more unexplainable emotions flowed out with her tears.

Amidst all this, one thing was certain: She was HEALING...

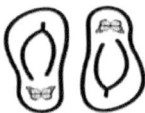

Minutes later, Dami stared with utmost curiosity at this mysterious young man beside her, who smiled back at her graciously.

When words finally remembered her, she asked the question she's been most curious about.

"Who are you?"

The young man's smile deepened as he watched the pretty young lady beside him; he was expecting the question.

"I'm a friend who's been waiting to hear your story."

Dami watched him in awe; she didn't get mad. She was stunned.

She wasn't feeling repulsive towards this stranger like she had been with many others who had tried to pry. Instead, she feels relaxed and comfortable around him.

In as much as she tried to understand this mystery, it was an undeniable reality that he meant no harm.

His words were like soothing ice on coals of fire to

her heart. She couldn't resist the urge to tell him all about herself and all that she'd been through. She wasn't willing to resist opening up her heart to Him. She already believed in Him.

Dami told him all that's been troubling and weighing her down for years, her diagnosis as a PTSD patient, how it's been tough living after her abuse and how she's thought about giving up on life for many years.

The young man listened with rapt attention, not interrupting as he watched her open up to him. Occasionally, he'd tap her hand gently and reassuringly when tears rolled out of her eyes, and she got lost for words while the memories of her past hit her hard in the process of telling her story.

When she was done, he finally started his mission.

"Dearest one, I bear a message from the throne of His Majesty, the Creator of life and all that's in it. The one who knows all things, the Supreme Being and the Controller of the entire universe.

I know all you've been through. I understand how firmly you've withstood it all. I want you to know that I've seen all your tears, and I've heard both the silent and spoken words and the meaning behind each drop. You're loved and greatly cherished. You're my precious daughter. I won't let you be in pain anymore. I've heard your family's prayers and cries, and I'm going to wipe away their tears. The chains of depression that'd held you down are now broken. You've been let loose from your captivities.

Greener pastures await you, my precious, and I have restored to you that glorious joy you once had. You've been healed perfectly and permanently.

Remember, I had loved you even before you were conceived and have known your end even from your beginning.

Wipe your tears, my child. I've never forsaken you and never will I.

You're my precious, always remember you're loved."

Dami couldn't control her outbursts as she continued to sob convulsively while she listened to all he said. She soon felt a tender, reassuring touch on her shoulder as she kept crying...

"What's wrong with her?"

"Hey, isn't it that weird girl from down the street? Why is she crying so convulsively on the highway?"

"Eyaah, it's probably gotten a grip on her totally. I heard she's suffering from PTSD, she's probably not sane anymore."

"Hurry! Call someone over. We probably need to take her to the psychiatric hospital."

A huge crowd had gathered around the usually quiet street. Hmm, how fast the wind bears tales...

Oblivious of what was going on around her, Dami

sat on the floor still weeping endlessly in gratitude over her miraculous healing and over the immense joy that was tugging at her heart. Her joyous heart was doing backflips out of excess joy. This feeling was too sweet to comprehend; she surely wouldn't want to be interrupted.

Only when the sound of an ambulance siren came blasting loudly in her ears did she become conscious of her environment.

Slowly, she peeled her eyes open only to see many pairs of unfamiliar eyes staring down with pity at her.

Where's the young man? How am I here? I was down that street a few minutes ago, conversing in that beautiful garden with that mysterious stranger. How is this possible?

Several thoughts ran through her mind as she looked around at the people watching her. Soon enough, she came to a sudden realization.

She'd just had a supernatural encounter!

She'd been in a trance just now!

Remembering the stranger's words again, tears flowed freely down her cheeks, and soon, she wasn't able to hold them back anymore as her cheeks broke into a wide grin. Immediately, she pulled down her hoodie, jumping up instantly and shouting in a loud, excited voice;

"Thank God I am healed! I'm free once again! I'm healed and free totally!"

The onlookers were shocked as they wandered amongst themselves. Many agreed she was now totally insane, while many were full of surprise and disbelief as they watched her. She was the weird psycho they'd known for several years; how could she ever be normal? To them, she was far too deep in her depression and insanity to ever become sane again.

Soon, several white-clothed medical personnel came and escorted her to the ambulance, insisting she needed an urgent medical checkup. Dami didn't resist. She knew better than any of them how perfectly sane she is.

Meanwhile, some onlookers had put a call across to Nina, asking her to hurry down here immediately as her younger sister had gone totally crazy and insane and was being taken to the hospital.

A panic-stricken Nina barged into the doctor's office, fearing and expecting the worst, only to be greeted by a shocking, glorious, unbelievable sight.

Sitting and discussing laughingly with the doctor was her younger sister, Dami.

Dami had always been beautiful, but the blinding pulchritude of her dearest sister at this moment made Nina believe instantly that Dami was healed.

Her wishes and prayers have been answered.

Needing no other explanations as tears of joy and gratitude clouded her eyes, she ran over to her and immediately engulfed her in a long passionate embrace.

"Nina I'm healed! I'm fine now, but they all find it hard to believe me. Seriously, I'm healed now. You believe me, right?"

Dami sobbed into the shoulders of her sister.

"I'm completely fine now that I feel so alive and extremely elated right now," she cried.

"I know, dearest, I know," Nina agreed immediately, not doubting her sister even once. She wrapped her arms tightly around her as tears kept falling down her cheeks.

The doctor watched, awestricken, the unbelievable scene before him. He's been Dami's special therapist and psychiatrist for many years. He was a witness when his former Boss diagnosed the little Dami with PTSD many years before the latter retired, handing over her file to him.

What he was witnessing right now was an undeniable miracle.

The two sisters were crying convulsively in each other's arms again, but this time, it wasn't out of pain but out of gratitude, relief, and excess joy.

They've fought, and they've conquered. Dami is Healed!!!

On the way back home, they delivered the good news to their parents. Mrs Helen and her husband received this information with great joy; they also freely shared the latest of their discoveries concerning Uncle Madi.

Uncle Madi got caught by his wife while sexually abusing their four-year-old daughter the same way he did to Dami and many others years ago. She turned him in to the police, and he was placed behind bars immediately after he was found guilty. His past and present crimes caught up with him as the police found evidence against him, both from his crimes of the past and even his recent ones. He was made to face the law and is being punished according to the laws of the country against such crimes.

Nina and Dami received this news and couldn't help returning all thanks to God for his glorious and decisive intervention in their lives. They, however, felt sorry for Uncle Madi's young wife and their little daughter. They, however, trust God to take care of them as he so pleases.

And for the first time in many years, Dami slept peacefully and soundly, even hearing that familiar humming sound she loves so much in her sleep.

She'd been rebirth'ed.

Esther Alex is an undergraduate of the Federal University of Technology who strives to inspire many through her pen. She's also the author of the short stories; Diary of Zoriana, Dear Future Husband, Finding Myself amongst others.

THE FACELESS KILLER

Pearl Soni

Tick Tok. Tick Tok.

The clock chimed twelve.

My face was flushed, and my body was trembling with fear. I tried to open my mouth to scream but was muted like a mime artist. Anxiety took over me. I wasn't far from a panic attack. If you ever wondered what it would feel like if you knew you were going to die in the next second, this is what it felt like.

A piece of paper is pretty worthless until it has words on it, and the paper in my hand was definitely not worthless at all.

It read:

Jane Barlowe aka Zuri Abara,

Hope this note has reached you well because after the moment you read this, there will be no peace in your life. Jane Barlowe? You must be wondering. She is you but not you. Tell me, Zuri, who was she then?

From this moment onwards, I hold the plug to your life. One secret, and the plug will be pulled.

P.S. Let's not tell Gramps about our little friendship.

Okay, Janie?

That night, I lay in bed, confused. *What did whoever this was want? Why me? And who in this world is Jane Barlowe?*

I stayed awake like an insomniac.

First of all, I didn't know what information this psycho wanted about Jane. Second, how exactly was I going to find out? Who was I going to ask?

And gradually, I threw myself down the rabbit hole.

My head was blasting the next morning like someone was pounding on it with a ten-kilogram hammer. My eyes were blood red. The note was still the only thought in my head, but I tried to push it aside.

It was 7:46 a.m., and I was about to be officially late in the next fourteen minutes. My irritating boss called me out at the staff meeting. Oh gosh, I cannot explain how much that man gets on my nerves. It's like a battle with him every day.

See, I am a passenger service agent. In easy terms, I must add, the person who gives you your boarding pass with a very fake smile.

I reached the airport and rushed to slip in without anyone noticing. A humongous line of passengers was already ready to make my not-so-great morning worse. But finally, after an extremely long day, I was done and was on my way home.

As I left the main building, a reflective screen

almost blinded me. The date was flashed on the screen.

15/6/2021

The second I read the date, I started feeling restless. My legs felt numb, and I fell to the ground with a thud. It became hard to keep my eyes open, and soon, I was unconscious. All I remember is that I saw a segment of something.

The sky was a scary grey, and the clouds were so close that they almost squeezed the life out of me. I was thirty-three thousand feet above the ground. The engine was roaring and gasping to breathe through the rain. There was chaos in the flight, and I heard a man beside me say:

"Please, God, I want to see those sweet eyes one more time. Don't take me already."

I couldn't see his face, but that's all I heard. Slowly, everything started getting mixed up, and soon, there was silence and a total blackout.

I woke up.

People were swarming like bees around me, trying to make sure I was okay. Some held out water bottles, and others started fanning me. I finally gathered myself and got up. I thanked the people for their concern and told them I was fine. But some of them became leeches and followed me to my car. It's not like I didn't appreciate their care, but I was stable enough to handle myself, so if they had just let me go, I wouldn't have died. People and I don't have a great relationship, so I try to avoid them, but that's a story for another day.

I thought about that dream, vision or whatever I saw that whole day. I started making dinner and accidentally mixed all the spices and burnt the food. I was not functioning properly. I hated seeing myself like this. So, all I ate was a bunch of snacks and a nice cup of cocoa. In the middle of enjoying my very scrumptious meal, the doorbell rang. Immediately, my eyes pulled themselves to the clock straight ahead of me.

11:24 p.m., it read.

Who was it at this hour? Maybe it was one of my nosy neighbours coming to inform me that they were going to have another party, so I shouldn't be concerned about the chaos that would follow. I unwillingly dragged myself to the door and peeked through the peephole.

There was no one.

So, I opened the door just to find a 4x6, almond coloured envelope on the dusty floor. I looked around for traces of a human but couldn't see anything, partially due to the dimly lit street that I lived on. I examined the suspicious item lying at my feet. I may have even tried to kick it a little. I had watched enough crime movies to know not to pick anything foreign without finding out what it is. There was nothing on it, so I just decided to pick it up. I was shivering as I opened it up. I was a piece of paper that looked like it was torn from a larger piece in a hurry. As I unfolded that note, it suddenly hit me that this was another note.

Another note!

I wanted to throw it on the floor and not look, but my curious*ness* didn't let me do that. I finally opened the note fully. And the thing my eyes went to, was the last line – '🖤'. It was that psycho again.

This time, it was a little different.

Knock, knock, Janie! It's me again. I thought you would take some time, but you're a fast responder. I'm proud of you. Now come on, it's time to spill what you saw at the airport.

By the way, just so you know, I have eyes on you everywhere and anywhere, so there will be no point in trying to hide anything from me. Understand? You will receive a text message in about seven seconds; respond to it or else... 🖤

I stood there, frozen. Exactly seven seconds later, I received that message, and it asked me just to type all that I saw and not question at all. And so that's what I did. Told them about the flight.

I couldn't explain what was happening to me and why, but one thing I knew was that if I took one wrong step, that would be the end of Zuri Abara's life.

There was silence from their side for a couple of days, so I moved on with my life, terrified of every step I took. I knew that psycho was always lurking in the corners of every place I ever went, and I felt so insecure. My heart was always racing.

Every small note passed around by my colleagues made me think that that was *The One*. I was internally dying with every passing second that I lived. This feeling was the worst. I couldn't focus on anything and messed up at work multiple times until my boss had to apologise to so many passengers. In the end, I also got shouted at. But the surprising thing was that the shouting didn't faze me. I stood there like a statue and just listened and agreed. No annoying feelings, no feelings whatsoever. My mind was filled with thoughts and blank at the same time.

Another normal day was over, and I was off to bed. I hadn't slept properly since the first note. I knew that night wasn't going to be any different. I tucked myself under the blanket; it was the only one that gave me warmth on these cold, fearful days.

I closed my eyes, hoping that I would sleep, even if it were for a minute. All I saw was pitch blackness, and all I heard were the street dogs having their usual midnight duel. In a few seconds, the world around me started fading out, and sleep took over me. I don't know exactly when I started dreaming, but I did.

I was on my way to the airport but not in my car, which was strange because I had never travelled in someone else's car. I reached the airport and started getting my luggage out of the boot. Again, this was very unusual. But then I realised that I was travelling, not going to my job. I walked with my two suitcases in a trolley to the security check-in.

I passed a reflective door and saw my reflection in it. I was wearing a baby-blue button-up dress. It looked vintage, and I had no idea why I was wearing it. I handed my passport to a deep sounding man at the security check. He opened the key and read my name.

"Miss Jane Barlowe?" he asked.

"Yes," I replied. As I walked inside, the dream started fading, and I could only hear an echo of the name Jane Barlowe.

I closed my ears and woke up in an instant.

It was Jane Barlowe.

I had heaps of questions ready if only someone had the answers. How was it even possible? Why was I dreaming from this vintage lady's perspective? These were just a couple of other thoughts added to my overthinking pile.

I knew I was going to get another note because, obviously, somehow, that person knew I had another dream. So, I continued my day as usual because 'usual' was praying for my life now. I made my morning coffee, and I was off to work.

I was done, and it was time for lunch. I went to a nearby subway and ordered my daily sub. But as my life was going downhill, nothing was in my favour. The guy who made my sub every day was on leave today. So, I had to interact with this kid-like intern. He asked so many questions that, at a point, I thought about leaving that place even if it meant I didn't get my sub. But I pushed through and got to the paying bit.

Finally, she handed me my lunch, and I flew out of that place like I never had. In my car, I let the humidity inside calm my overly frustrated self before forcing my windows open. I hurriedly opened the wrapping on my sub, and I was about to crumble it up and toss it away when my eyes caught a glimpse of the writing on the corner of the wrapping. Before I even read it, I just wanted to confirm it was one of those notes. So, I straight went to the end, and yes, it was.

I flung the car door open and ran towards the subway place. I opened the door with all my energy only to find that the girl who served me was not there. I asked the man who was now there about her, but he just said that there was no one else there except him. I was baffled. I knew I was not daydreaming because she actually handed me the sub, and I had it in my hands. I tried to ask again, but the man just gently told me to go away as he had a long line of customers. So, I walked away, trying to figure out this situation.

Was that girl the one behind the notes? Or was she just a pawn used to throw me off? I didn't know, and there was nothing I could do to find out. The least I could do was to read the note. So, I slumped back in the driver's seat and read:

Enjoying a sub? It's nice to see you enjoy something while I'm looking for answers. Jane. Jane. Jane. Let's talk about that dream. What made you close your ears in the middle of a silent night? Let's have a friendly chat about this. Write your dream on this paper and give it to the black-hooded man you see in your backseat. Don't be scared; he's our friend, too.

P.S. Don't bother finding out who that sweet little girl who served you was. As we speak, her death certificate is being printed. 🖤

As soon as I finished reading, I felt a tap on my left shoulder. My heart almost fell out. I didn't want to look behind, so I waited. The man started tapping the handrest at equal intervals, almost as if he was counting down seconds. I quickly grabbed a pen from the glove compartment and started writing about my dream. As soon as I was done, I knew I had to see this man once, so I turned to him to hand him the paper. But, to my disappointment, he had a clown mask on. I wasn't much surprised as it's very common for criminals to cover their faces, and this one was no amateur not to do that.

My bare sub that was on a tissue on the seat beside me was waiting to be eaten. I picked it up and stuffed my mouth with big bites without even realising. If there was an anxiety scale, I must have exceeded the limit by then. I was just staring at the steering wheel and trying to process everything that had just happened. All of a sudden, I heard a fairly loud 'ding' from my phone. I came out of my trance and jumped slightly out of my seat. It was a message.

Finally, you know who Jane is. That took a while, but I'm happy now. You know the drill if you get more information. 🖤

Another 'ding'

This time, it was a useless message from my service

provider asking me to update my subscription to a 'cheaper' and 'faster' one. I love how they lie to you when it's the same thing you already have.

I was honestly just too tired of this person. I wanted to escape. I wanted to go back to my life. At least I was happy then. I didn't give the text another thought because I already had enough on my mind. I just drove back to work and continued my routine.

As I left work that day, my boss, for the very first time, came up to me and asked me if I was okay. Life was seriously giving me surprises. Since when was my boss, Mr Joseph, concerned if I was fine? I brushed him off, telling him that I'd just been having a few intense headaches, so I couldn't quite concentrate. He was settled by hearing that and left me to leave.

I drove home, and the evening seemed just as low as me. It was drizzling, and the gloomy clouds caved in. I was halfway home when I met a red signal. I stopped and just stared at the fiery red light. Soon, I felt myself sitting upright and all warm, and my eyes shut.

There was fire everywhere, burning clothes and cremating people. Endless screams were all that my ears could hear. It was a horrific scene. The pilot was trying really hard to stabilize the plane, but it just wasn't working. All the air hostesses were trying to give fake hope to all the passengers, and all of us didn't know what we were doing.

At that moment, I felt like that was the end. There was no way that I would get out of there alive. I could see the land approaching, and no sign of us flying further on. All I could do was pray for my life. I decided not to look outside the window because that stressed me out more. Instead, I just closed my eyes and hugged myself tightly, thinking about all the beautiful moments that life had given me. As a few seconds passed, I heard a thud.

The plane had crashed, and, in a few milliseconds, I saw the front of the plane being squished and compressed. It wasn't long before the end of my life. And so, I just closed my eyes, hoping for a miracle amid this tragedy. The scene blacked out, and there I awoke.

Jane Barlowe was dead. This is how she died in a plane crash. Why was I getting this dream? Just before I got my answer to that question, I remembered that Jane was wearing a charm bracelet on her hand that had a small dolphin charm on it. And I had the same on mine. Was this just a coincidence, or did it mean something?

I drove ahead and reached home. I rushed inside and just sat on the sofa. I thought about every possible reason we both wore the same charm. But in the end, I came to no conclusion. I went to get myself a glass of water to ease myself. On the counter, I saw a lined piece of paper that had yet had another note written on it.

Congratulations, Jane, or should I say Zuri? Does that even make a difference? It seems like you have concluded. Oh Jane, don't be so worried. Jane is you, and you are Jane. And that wasn't so hard, was it? By the way, that charm isn't just any charm. That's exactly what I want. But of course, I couldn't ask directly because what kind of decent behaviour is that. A little trauma was needed. And so here you are. So, hand me that charm, and you shall be free.

Place it right outside your door, and I'll take it from there. 🖤

Ok, so this whole experience was just about that psycho wanting a charm? Why would that person make me go through so much and literally ruin my life just for that? I stopped thinking and I just went to place my charm outside the door. I placed it on the doormat and was just looking around to see anybody. Just as I was going inside, I felt someone grab me by the waist.

A black glove held my waist, and I felt a knife at my throat.

I was trembling with fear; I had no clue what was happening. But just in a few seconds, the grip loosened. I looked behind only to find a masked figure standing in front of me with a bloody knife in their hand.

Whoever that person was had just stabbed the person who was holding me. I don't know why, and I don't know how. But it just happened.

He walked by me and whispered in my ear. "Thank you. Thank you, Jane. And you're welcome, Zuri. I am psycho, but I wouldn't have killed you. We're friends, remember? 🖤."

Then vanished into thin air.

That is when it hit me.
I was Jane Barlowe in my previous life.

Pearl Soni is a Kenyan student who believes we should be the reason someone smiles.

BONUS STORY

THE FALLOUT
Agnes Kay-E

Eka hurried home, almost having an accident on the Calabar-Itu road twice. The house she'd just struck a deal on was her husband, Ettebòng's dream house. Not hers, but they had each other, which meant she'd be forced to go with him to live in Lagos. She lived all her life on Uwang-Iba road, so it was a bother. It was a real bother, a worse bother than her inability to be a mother. She had the comfort of her cousins' children and his uncles' children. It wouldn't matter with Ettebòng by her side.

Eka's bladder sought respite, but she couldn't register its need, not with the great news she had. The good news opened doors to great sex, a feat that was last achieved a few months before the first lockdown. She hadn't seen Ettebòng in weeks, and she was at the peak of sensual heat. The lockdown had meant they barely saw each other, and when they did, they were too busy. To worsen it, some members of Ettebòng's family had made her home their refuge. In her hopes, she cleared her schedule just as he'd done his so that there'd be no interference for the next three weeks. She had gone out of her way to buy tickets for

Ettebòng's mother and youngest sister to go for a long holiday in Barbados, where his uncle had decided to study, only he went on to get a girl pregnant and abandon his purpose. It meant one less set of fees to worry about, which was a relief.

Eka noticed a few things at the entrance while her husband's brother tried to wrangle his way into getting the keys to her *Range Rover*. For some reason, anything belonging to her husband belonged to his family. Her family had been kept in awe of having a generous husband. She frowned, wondering what could have made Kiki forget the food on the stove again. She had gotten rid of Joshua, the gateman with whom Kiki was tangled in romantic acrobatics. The new gateman had discarded a bucket of soap suds by Ettebòng's car. It was then she noticed that there were two buses in her compound. She opened the door, and her nostril was christened with the smell of camphor and fermented cassava.

Eka tried to reach the light and discovered it was on but was obscured by the number of people in the room. She recognised some from the wedding she'd attended last weekend, elders from both sides of the family as they were from neighbouring villages. They looked to the centre of the second sitting room, so she inched closer to find out what had engulfed their interest.

In the centre of the epic interest was her mother flanked by her stepfather and husband's cousin who had just returned from South Africa. To her left was

Ettebòng, who was flanked by her sister, who had been missing for months, and an empty chair.

Eka sighed with relief on seeing her sister and nudged through the crowd to meet her. Seeing a baby in her sister's arms, she assumed it was the reason her sister had disappeared. She didn't mind if her sister had a child, just a little disappointed as she absconded when she had one year left with Ritman University.

"Eyen Ekanmi, where have you been? You didn't do well, o!" Eka said and hurried towards her sister, but as soon as she was close, her mother-in-law blocked her path, shaking her head disapprovingly and nudging her towards the vacant chair. Used to her mother-in-law's way, she went to the chair with an amused smile. She politely greeted everyone and received mutters and murmurs. Her mother's response was the only one that bothered her; it didn't have the optimistic, upbeat characteristics that she was used to.

"What's with the gloom? it's not like anybody has died."

"That would have been better news," Ettebòng retorted in a whisper.

Eka appraised him and sneered cheekily. *What could be so bad about having a baby?*

She could tell it was her sister's; the glow of a new mother was written all over her. She didn't understand her mother's gloom when she should be happy that her daughter wasn't barren, or as her mother liked to say, 'out of babies'. She could understand her husband's disappointment since they practically raised her sister like their own. She didn't care much for the rest of the family members in the room; as far as she was concerned, their gloom was misplaced. Perhaps their gloom was because there was no man attached to her sister's limb.

"Imaima, she only had a child o," Eka said softly, touching his thigh.

Ettebòng stiffened.

Eka pulled her hand back to herself and asked in a worried voice, "What's the problem?"

Ettebòng's mother got up and sauntered towards her. "You know how me I like to remove the bandage one time," she said, waving her hand dramatically.

Ettebòng glared at his mother, who responded with a hiss, and an eye roll, poking the air between herself and Eka; she continued, "Eka, your sister has done what you can't."

"Obviously," Eka muttered under her breath.

"What did you say?" her mother-in-law asked, her glare furious.

Eka pursed her lips, shrugged, and said nonchalantly, "Nothing o."

"Your sister here…" Ettebòng's mother danced and added. "Has brought a smile to my face, our faces, is that not so?" she asked the people in the room, and they muttered in agreement. "Now I can join my husband, knowing that his lineage has not ended with him."

Eka frowned, and then a daunting realisation caused a gasp to escape her lips. "Wha-at?" she asked in a strangled voice.

"Imami, it was a mis...mis...take," Ettebòng stammered.

Irritated, Ettebòng's mother asked, "Why are you explaining?"

Ettebòng shifted in his seat.

"My sister. My youngest sister has lived in this house since she was a child."

"Eka, please hear me out," Ettebòng started in Ibibio. "I'll never..."

Eka stared at his fair hand on her knee as if it was an oversized worm and pushed it off with her purse."

Someone cleared their throat. A few sticks struck the marble floor.

"Ehem, that's enough," Ette Ekambayak, the oldest man from Ettebòng's clan who was related to no one in particular, or no one they knew of, started, paused, and continued, "You can sort yourselves out later. As the young girl is yet unmarried and has agreed to marry Ettebòng Essien Uyak this morning, and the dowry has been collected this morning also. Why were we invited?"

"I wanted us to celebrate these new additions," Ettebòng's mother mumbled, doing another triumphant dance around the space in the middle of the room, reminding Eka that they'd yet to replace the centre table, which was broken months before the first lockdown. "Where is our baby's sister? Go and bring her." Ettebòng's mother did another dance and stuck her tongue out at Eka.

Ettebòng's elder brother sang as he processed forward with the baby. He didn't have children himself. It's good he said that he was *forgiven* because none of his wives lasted long enough to give him one. He didn't cast a glance in her direction, but he couldn't, he wouldn't dare, not after he tried to make advances towards her during the lockdown. His broken teeth were enough warning.

Eka sneered at the man who had spoken, grimaced at her mother-in-law, inwardly shook her head at her mother and sister and pursed her lips to fight the early onset of tears. She watched the proceedings – they were naming the babies.

It wasn't a dream. She pinched herself on occasion, willing it to be a nightmare and that each pinch would wake her up. Everyone seemed to have fallen into a spell that made her an outsider, like Sam Wheat in *Ghost,* staring at his body on the ground and calling for help. She couldn't call for help, not from this lot; she would get none. Most of them were under the impression that she had cast a spell on her husband to keep her as his only wife without children.

Blood rushed to Eka's ears, banishing the sounds around her. Whatever the deliberation, she could only see moving lips, nodding heads, shaking heads, swinging fists, chest striking, but the ones that stood out to her, where Ettebòng's mother's hands tucked in her armpits, while her mother's arms were folded beneath her breasts - one stance of disapproval and the other solemn agreement. Summoning strength to her legs, she got up and made her way up the stairs to the shelter of her bedroom.

Eka frowned at her bed for a while, wondering if the forbidden act had ever happened on it. She shied away from her bed, went to the vanity chair, and stared blankly at her reflection.

A long while later, Eka's mother walked in without knocking. It broke her heart, for, in the thirty-three years of her marriage to Ettebòng, it was the first time anyone else had walked into their bedroom. To make it worse, her mother sat on the bed.

Not ready to cry in front of her mother, she sucked on her upper lip.

"Em... Adiaha mmi, please don't be offended," Eka's mother started in Ibibio and then continued in English. "What happened wasn't supposed to happen, but it has happened. She's your sister o! Hmmm." Her mother fell silent for a long time, and she thought her mother had left until she added, "I think it is a good thing –"

Eka inhaled sharply.

"What if it was with another woman? You see the kind of mother-in-law you have; she will just kick you out. How will we survive? Where will you live? It's a good thing. With your sister here –"

"Here?" Eka asked in a whisper.

"Ehen, nawh. The child is your husband's own, isn't it?"

"So, it's ok that my sister slept with my husband."

"Ekaette, that is in the past nawh. The baby is already here. You love children, you can manage. Wouldn't you like to be a mother for real? Your sister will go back to school and finish, and you will play the role of a mother. God knows that baby will need a real mother."

Eka scoffed in shocked surprise. Her disappointment was unfathomable. She had always known her mother to be callous, but this was beyond evil. Did she truly have no one on her side? If she'd been under the illusion of having a mother's love as Uduak Eyo, her best friend since they could walk, had implied, then she was surely thinking straight now. There was no love there.

"Eka-Eka," Ettebòng's voice boomed cheerfully as he greeted his mother-in-law.

"Eyen mmi (*my son*)," Eka's mother cried excitedly, slanted her head and whispered, "Usuk, usuk. Softly, softly."

Usuk, usuk. Eka scoffed again.

"Imami," Ettebòng started and exhaled heavily. "I'm sorry. It wasn't meant to happen."

Eka exhaled as softly as she could. She'd been too disappointed and wanted to dwell on her pain alone. She closed her eyes, but they snapped open the instant his perfume wafted into her nostrils, the perfume she'd gone out of her way to get at *The Perfume Shop* and almost tripped on black ice twice. It wasn't like she wanted to be in the USA at the time; Ettebòng wanted to attend a wedding and needed her for moral support. Anywhere Ettebòng went, she tagged along. It wasn't a problem because she could run her business from anywhere in the world if it had the Internet. It was one of the things Ettebòng claimed to love about their marriage - no child to tie them down.

"Imami, please don't be offended. Please forgive me."

She guffawed and stared incredulously at him. "I shouldn't be offended?"

Ettebòng was uncomfortable with her silence. more so, with the timbre of her voice as low as it was. He could almost feel the anger in it.

She got up then. She'd heard rumours about his cheating on her, but she chucked it to the fact that men weren't satisfied with one type of soup. She didn't believe it, but sometimes a spell of rumour was better served with the illusion of belief.

"Thirty-five years."

Ettebòng winced. Eka had never called him Ettebòng. Ettebòng

"Thirty-five. And you decided that my sister will be the person I'll share your penis with." Eka inhaled sharply, then emphasised, "My sister. The girl that you didn't want under your roof because it would, in your words, 'crap our lifestyle'. A girl that grew up in your house. How old is she?"

Ettebòng exhaled despairingly.

"How old?" Eka snapped.

Startled, Ettebòng retorted, "Twenty-two."

"Of which she lived fifteen of in your house. Would that not make you a paedophile?"

"Imami," Ettebòng admonished in a choked voice.

"You're still more than half her age. Do you need me to tell you your age?"

"Imami," Ettebòng pleaded. "I'll never cheat on you and –"

"But you did. With my sister."

"Half-sister."

Eka spun to face him, squinting. Was he really trying to justify his actions? She grimaced. Why was she calmly talking to him? Was she not the one that kicked Ettebòng's elder brother in the balls and offered him an ice pack a few months ago? Was she not the one who'd sent Ernest Obóigha to the hospital with a concussion because he'd made advances at her a few hours ago? She shook her head, held it, and stumbled.

Ettebòng caught her, but she shoved him away and steadied herself before heading to the bathroom, where she locked the door and sagged to the floor.

Eka ran a bath and stared at it, reminiscing on her marriage. She met Ettebòng when two schools came to use her school's football field. His school was an all-boys school, which had attracted a lot of attention because there had never been a scandal from it. She had just been made senior prefect and was still basking in the euphoria of the marginal win and had accepted to go to the school compound on a Saturday.

Her heart melted as soon as she set eyes on him; he'd walked onto the field so casually that she was certain that he was going to be worse than the goalkeeper he was replacing. He wasn't. He blocked all the balls in the penalty shootout. It had never been heard of. He was an instant sensation. Their relationship became the next best thing. They'd been inseparable from that day until now.

Eka recalled her argument with Uduak, her best friend, and smiled ruefully. They had fought because of Ernest Obóigha. Ernest was someone she'd met at the University of Benin during her Masters. Ernest Obóigha knew she was married, but that didn't stop him. He chased her everywhere, even though he believed in the sanctity of marriage. He was her only friend in that city, but Ettebòng didn't like it, and she told him and stopped communicating with him. But that morning, while she was waiting to hear from a realtor in Lagos, the one that could possibly get her the house Ettebòng loved.

Eka had whacked Ernest with a paperweight; an accident - Ernest had kissed her and, instead of apologising, professed love. Startled by the effect of his kiss, she pulled back. As she did, her swivel chair spun. Because her hands were stretched out, she swept most of the things on her table in his direction. Ernest was at eye level with the table because he was still on his knees, so the paperweight connected with his temple. He stumbled to his feet, nursing his temple. At the same time, Uduak barged in, startling them. In pulling back, he hit his head against the filing cabinet she had forgotten to close and fell forward and was flat on the floor. If Uduak hadn't been by the door, she would have run away because he didn't look like he was breathing. And if Uduak hadn't barged in to ask if he was successful, she wouldn't have guessed how he'd found her.

Here she was giving her all to a man who thought her heart was *okoso* while another man pined for her, and she was doing the same to his heart.

Oh Ettebòng, a baby no longer 'craps your style'.

Tears trickled down Eka's face, but she wasn't sobbing. It was almost as if she had done all of it in the early years of her marriage. She'd endured her mother-in-law's abuse and bridled her tongue because she wanted Ettebòng to be happy. She had tolerated the constant intrusions of his family, tolerated the constant financial quests of her family and his. She'd had eleven abortions to suit Ettebòng's desires. For some reason, contraceptives had never worked for her. The first four abortions were because they weren't married, then it became 'will the children eat sand?' She'd done enough of it to make her only reaction a wince when the doctor widened her cervix to poke around. Pregnancy had stopped happening, and she'd come to accept it as a reward for her past actions.

All her adult life had been about what Ettebòng wanted. Nothing happened in Uyo without Ettebòng's knowing. He swayed with the rhetorics and in the plights of Akwa Ibom State's elitist on her backbone. She had spent over thirty years making him look good. Now, she is meant to swallow her pride yet again and play mother to his child by her sister. Was she always going to hide under the elusive shadow of her husband?

Sighing, Eka got up and left the bathroom. She must have been there a long time because her bedroom was dark, the windows were open, and Ettebòng was asleep. She scoffed, picked up her phone and dialled a number.

"Uduak, when are you leaving town?" Eka asked, nodded at intervals, then added, "Let's talk."

She glanced at Ettebòng, then at her pillow, and exhaled sharply as she picked up her purse and car keys, then glanced at the time. A minute to six. Dinner time. She slapped her head, remembering that she was supposed to take Kiki to the bus park.

Eka walked to the landing and called Kiki.

"Ma!" Kiki cried and slammed a few doors before reaching her.

"Are you ready?"

"Yes ma," Kiki replied and curtsied.

Frowning at Kiki's outfit, she decided to give Kiki a forever holiday.

"I hope you didn't forget anything o!" she mumbled as she walked down the rest of the stairs.

"No ma," Kiki said and curtsied again.

"Take your things to the car. Hurry up, please."

"Eka, I thought you were sleeping," Eka's mother said groggily as she walked towards her.

Well, I'm not. Eka hung around the edge of the stairs. She didn't want to go to the part of the house where she had been scandalised. Her sister sat in the same place she'd been, now dressed differently.

"Eka, is there any food? Your sister needs to eat, you know, for the sake of the baby."

"She knows where the kitchen is," Eka retorted in a crisp tone.

"What about Kiki?" Eka's mother asked. "She can help."

Eka inhaled sharply. Kiki settled beside her at the same time with two pieces of luggage. Eka was glad she had gotten it for Kiki, or they'll have had to go to the airport with raffia bags.

"Eh," Eka's mother scratched her ear. "Where is Kiki going?"

"I go home, ma. It's Easter holiday, ma," Kiki said, smiling sheepishly.

"Eh! She goes on holidays too?"

"Mama, I've got to take Kiki to the park," Eka said, slithered between her mother and Kiki and walked briskly towards the door.

"But we'll need a room, food —"

Eka clenched her teeth and exhaled slowly. "Your daughter knows her way around this house."

"When are you coming back? Should I lock the door?"

Eka turned to face her mother, her face bearing no expression.

"I'll not lock the door but come back early o. The dark is never safe, especially for a woman."

Eka ignored her mother and hurried away because staying longer may make her give her mother some stripes. As she couldn't beat her mother, she could unleash words that she wouldn't take back, but she wasn't about to give her the relief from guilt.

"Aunty mi," Kiki started, "You have passed the park o!"

"I know. I'm dropping you at the airport."

"Aunty!"

"You'll be going by plane."

"Me!?"

"Yes, my dear."

"Like for feem," Kiki writhed excitedly in the seat beside her. "Tó! Like rich people."

Eka smiled. *Yes, like rich people.*

At the airport, she managed to wrangle a flight ticket twice its price for Kiki. Since Ibom Air was used in a movie, it had become incredibly difficult to get a ticket without booking early. As Kiki readied to board, she sat down, pulled out her cheque book and began to scribble, then folded the cheque leaflet in Kiki's hand.

"Don't open it until you get to your house. I'll call you in a few hours. Abasiama will pick you up."

Kiki squealed and jumped on her. She untangled Kiki's slender arms a while later and mumbled, "Safe journey."

"Thank you, ma," Kiki retorted and joined the departure queue. She watched Kiki and continued to stare at the now vacant spot. She would miss Kiki. Kiki had a flair for the dramatic but always made her smile, except when she burnt food; she turned the house to soot when she did, and every piece of exposed clothing upstairs would carry the smell, even after a couple of washes. Thinking of burnt food made her remember her mother's need for her to provide food for her sister, a girl who'd ridiculed her a few hours ago. She wouldn't have minded, but her mother needed a taste of her medicine.

She shrugged off the irritating buzzing until she realised that it came from her purse. It was her phone. Uduak was calling. She quickly picked it up, murmuring;

"Sorry, I'm on my way."

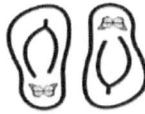

She didn't return home until morning. Walking in, she found Ettebòng's mother bathing one of the babies while her mother dried the other.

"Where are you coming from? Where have you been? You wanted to kill your mother?" Ettebòng's mother said in one breath, sighed and cooed to the baby, who was now crying. The tiny thing in front of his buttocks informed her it was the boy. She wondered if he was going to be like his father. She recalled Uduak's advice after they'd returned from visiting Ernest in the hospital and shook her head. She had spent the rest of the night thinking of Uduak's advice about the babies and Ernest. The ideas had begun to make sense as she drove home. It would be a fresh start. Following Uduak's plan would require leaving no stone unturned.

"Eka!" Ettebòng's mother's voice thundered into her reverie.

Eka frowned at Ettebòng's mother.

"Come nawh! Come and carry the baby. I need to use the toilet."

Eka carried the crying baby, and as soon as he was in the crook of her arm, he fell silent.

"Wow! He's been crying all night but, in your arms, ..." Ettebòng's mother's voice trailed off.

Eka squinted at it. It would have been her son over a decade or two ago. How old would the first or the last have been? Thirty-five and twenty-two. She shuddered at how accurately she had remembered something she had put out of her mind.

The baby made suckling sounds. She tucked a finger in his hand then walked to the chair she'd sat in through the scarring discovery, offered the baby a wry smile and mumbled incoherent words.

Your father betrayed me, but I can't see his betrayal in you. Eka caught a glint of light and slanted her head to see her sister.

"I think it's hungry," Eka said, getting up.

Eka watched her sister scurry towards her and curtsy. She handed the baby to her sister, who went to sit opposite her and plugged the baby's mouth with her nipple. Her sister had never curtsied to her.

What is it supposed to mean? That she was going to be the underling? My co-wife?

Suddenly cold, she massaged her arms.

Would I feel any different if she was another woman? Did I groom my sister and mould her into my husband's spec? How could I have been so blind to my husband's promiscuity?

"Sister?"

Eka wondered if 'sister' was still appropriate. Feeling nauseous, she got up and made her way towards the only space she could almost claim as hers. As she did, she knew she could never remain in the house. It no longer held anything for her. She came to a halt at the edge of the stairs and struggled to breathe; Ettebòng was standing in the same spot, the step before the last where he usually stood to welcome her if he returned home before her; a place he probably would have been standing to greet her if yesterday's event hadn't occurred. It was where he stood to kiss her with ease; she was almost a foot taller than him.

"I need to pass," Eka said in a strangled voice.

"Imami," Ettebòng started.

"You've lost the right to call me that," Eka snapped, gesturing at her sister.

Ettebòng stretched his hand towards Eka, her phone in it. She grabbed it, and he grabbed her hand. She used her free hand to swat at his.

Eka left the house that evening and returned in the morning for the rest of the week. In the house, she hid behind phone calls.

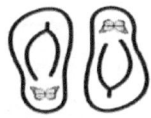

A week later, on Saturday, she had slept into the night and missed her usual exit. She was woken by the babies; they'd been crying for some time. She checked on them, mainly out of curiosity, because Ettebòng's mother and his sister had discovered the tickets and slipped out of town. Eka's mother had returned home because her husband had begun to complain about her absence. Ettebòng had the sudden urge to attend a gala in Lagos and had left that evening.

Saturday evening, their neighbour's speakers weren't blasting profane symphonies for some reason, which was unusual. Her sister was missing. Initially, she had assumed her sister had slept off in the toilet or the living room. She became hysterical when she couldn't find her sister until she noticed her sister's phone wasn't at her bedside.

To cast out any form of suspicion, she decided to call the phone, and a male voice picked up; she could hear music in the background. She shook her head, set the phone down and picked one crying baby at a time.

"I hope you're not as demanding as your father," Eka cooed. She sang the babies to sleep like she'd been doing for every child she had cared for as a teenager, as an adult with her cousin's children and Ettebòng uncles' children. She was surprised that her sister had gone to a party or the club. It was the one thing they'd often fought about.

As she sang the girl to sleep, Uduak called, and she recalled Uduak's advice. As she pondered on it, her heart beat faster until she was heaving. Everything was working like Uduak had suggested, only she hadn't orchestrated anything.

Deciding to act and not think, she spoke first: "Uduak, I need you."

An hour passed, and Uduak was in her house, but she didn't come alone.

Eka frowned at Ernest, who shrugged, a bandage still rimmed his head.

"Ernest, these babies are coming with me," Eka emphasised.

Ernest blinked. He knew the implication of what she was doing and hesitated, but as he opened his mouth to speak, Uduak raised a hand, asking:

"Do you still want to be with her?"

"Of-of course," Ernest stammered. "What do I need to do?"

Eka gestured at two suitcases, a laptop bag, and two baby bags.

"I'll take them to the car."

"Yes, you do that," Uduak said and waited until he was out of sight then turned to Eka with concern. "Are you sure you want to do this?"

"Are you chickening out now?"

"No. But this is you we're talking about."

"Ettebòng has caused a disturbance in my soul that can't be rescinded. This is cause and effect, my friend." Eka wasn't sure about her plan until then. She would make a good mother. She was going to take her place and everything with it. She wasn't going to work in another man's shadow. She was her own woman.

"I just needed you to say it," Uduak said, hugged her friend and went to carry the two baby bags.

Ernest returned, slung Eka's laptop over his shoulder and, holding onto the remaining suitcase, he stretched a free hand to her. "Ready?"

Eka exhaled as the weight of her decision fell on her. Determined to go ahead, she nodded. Uduak had agreed to help her sell the house. She had given Uduak her car keys. As soon as she was on the plane, it would be hers.

She had not expected to be ushered into a private jet. Ernest's client had lent it to him for two hours. She slanted her head to find Ernest staring adoringly at her and remembered how pleasantly his lips had felt on hers. She may fall in love again, but at least they knew where they stood. She glanced out of the window just as Ernest took her hand in his. His touch sent shivers down her midriff.

Yes, we could start with sex.

Ernest's phone beeped. He scrolled through it, chuckled and explained, "We're going on another lockdown."

She winked at the babies.

Yes, we will start with sex.

Agnes Kay-E is a Nigerian author based in England and the author of sixteen books, including Something New and Blossom in Winter, a bestseller. She writes contemporary fiction of vast genres, fantasy, and new age fiction. Her latest is Aguiyi, a play to be released in 2023. She is presently working on another contemporary fiction. In her spare time, she sings and writes music.

OTHER KEP TITLES

Ogu & Other Stories

Notes on Love

Rebirth

Oops!

Bound by Fate

Sink or Swim

Loving Nigeria

CONTACTS

Thank you for purchasing this book.
I hope you enjoyed it.

Please leave a review of what you thought of this book at your favourite retailer.

For more, let's meet at any of these places.

Facebook: https://www.facebook.com/kepressng
Instagram: https://www.instagram.com/kepressng
For newsletters: https://www.kepressng.com

ABOUT US

Kemka Ezinwo Press (KEP) Ltd is an African publishing company with the vision of broadening the power of African literary works and compositions. Our aim is to remind the world that we're avid readers and to combat the self-imposed superstition that Africans don't read.

Our core values are Excellence, Collaboration, Discovery, & Generosity.

To launch our official opening, we decided to introduce the KepressNG Anthology prize, a collection of short stories from debut and veteran authors with African lineage. We incorporated our Vision of developing and increasing African literature by making it a competition for the selection of the best story.

The KepressNG Anthology prize is designed for all writers, though not restricted to them, to write stories that they'd hope to read. Our stories matter, and who better than us to tell our stories? Societies change, and the most affected are the young.

2026 ANTHOLOGY

Attention all writers of African heritage - this is your moment to shine. The 2026 Kepressng Anthology Prize will officially open for submissions on May 29, 2026. Whether you're a published author or just beginning your journey, we invite you to explore this chance to showcase your talent.

Ten lucky winners will:
~Be published in an anthology.

This year, the competition features four categories:
~ VINE
~ LILY
~ JUVENILE
~ OAK.

The theme for each category is the same as the title, but it's up to you to interpret it however you wish – literally, figuratively, or creatively.

GUIDELINES

Entry is free and open to all African and those of African descent.
~ Your work must be original, unpublished and not AI-generated.
~Your entry must be in English and fictional.
~ You can submit only one entry per category.
~ All entries must be submitted in MS Word format, double line spaced in TIMES ROMAN font.
~ Your name must not appear in the body of the story.
~ The entry must be between 5,000 and 10,000 words.
~ Your submission email title must be as follows:
CATEGORY TITLE - YOUR STORY TITLE - YOUR NAME (PSEUDONYM).
~ All entries must be received by Midday of October 11, 2026.
~ The winners will be announced six weeks after the last day of submission. (A Change of date will be communicated.)

This is an incredible opportunity to have your work recognised, gain exposure, and most importantly, join a vibrant community of African writers! We can't wait to see your interpretation of these themes.

Send your submissions & FAQs to kemkaezinwo.press@gmail.com.

Good luck.

www.ingramcontent.com/pod-product-compliance
Lightning Source LLC
LaVergne TN
LVHW041846070526
838199LV00045BA/1468